A SHADOW
FROM
THE HEAT

MARGARET E. KELCHNER

BEACON HILL PRESS OF KANSAS CITY
KANSAS CITY, MISSOURI

LR DT AH WW

Copyright 1994
by Beacon Hill Press of Kansas City

ISBN: 083-411-5158

Printed in the
United States of America

Cover Design: Crandall Vail
Cover Illustration: Keith Alexander

10   9   8   7   6   5   4   3   2   1

About the Author

Margaret E. Kelchner was born in Palatka, Fla., the only daughter of Alexander Steen Fox (son of Camden C. and Nan [Sparks] Fox) and Nina Marguerita [Blackmer] Fox. Her father was a printer/pressman and her mother a practical nurse.

Caught in the grip of the Great Depression, the family migrated to Dayton, Ohio, where her father pursued a career in the printing business, and Margaret grew up to the smell of printer's ink and the sound of presses.

Her mother instilled in their four children at an early age a love for literature, and a weekly trip to the library was a priority. Each child was encouraged to choose books that were challenging and entertaining. Often the family carried home "a stack." Margaret was especially intrigued with the encyclopedias that "opened up the world beyond her door."

Married to a minister, and an ordained minister herself, Margaret has instilled in her own three children the same love for good books. Each of them has pursued advanced degrees and each has developed impressive home libraries. Margaret believes good literature is the best gift she can give her grandchildren and strives to "wrap a good book" for their birthdays and Christmases.

In her career in the church, Margaret has served in Christian education both at the state and national levels. She has contributed articles to the periodicals of several denominations.

Recognizing the need for wholesome and entertaining Christian books, Margaret turned to writing novels based on historical fact. *Father of the Fatherless,* her first novel, was released in 1993.

The author shares briefly her philosophy for writing fiction: "A book should not only be exciting and entertaining, with mystery, humor, and intrigue but have an underlying Christian message." She explains that her purpose is to "set the reader down" in a story in which people of the past work their way out of adversity in a practical, believable manner, while conveying the sense, "Yes, life is really worth living!"

1

A SCORCHING DESERT SUN had shone down from the cloudless sky all day. Heat waves radiated from the parched earth, giving ghostly shapes to the giant cactus and mesquite trees claiming existence in the rocky soil. The pungent odor of stunted creosote bushes filled the hot dry air. In the distance, a dust devil twisted and whirled eerily as it danced across the desert floor, disappearing and reappearing, sucking dust high into the atmosphere.

"No wonder they call them dust devils!" the rider grunted out loud with a grimace. The hot dry air burned his nostrils and throat, making speech difficult. It had been so long since he had heard a human voice, he was startled to hear his own.

He sat listless in the saddle, the reins laying loose over the pommel. His canteen had long been empty, and he knew his life depended on the big, chestnut-colored horse he rode. The animal's uncanny sense of smell for water was their only hope. If they did not find it soon, they would perish here.

Squinting up at the sun, he realized there was little daylight left to find water and shelter. It had been a long, torturous day and both man and beast were anticipating its end. He dreaded to leave the fragile shade where the horse had paused to catch its wind but knew they must move on.

The surefooted mount picked his way to the top of a low ridge heading into a canyon. With a quiet snort, he halted abruptly and stood looking off into the deepening shadows to the right, head high, ears pointed. Aroused from his weary stupor, the man sat alert and motionless, suddenly aware that he was silhouetted against the sky.

"You're right, Rowdy," he said in a hoarse whisper, "I feel it too—an' I'm making a good target up here."

He slipped his rifle from its scabbard and eased himself to the ground where he stood listening, ears straining to hear the slightest sound. Through narrowed, bloodshot eyes he searched the rough terrain ahead for any sign of movement, gazing long into the deepening shadows of the rocks.

Satisfied there was no immediate danger, he led Rowdy slowly into the darkness at the base of the canyon wall. High cliffs above his head were lit up in bold relief from the last golden rays of the sun, while night came quickly in the dark recesses of this wilderness place.

He had gone only a short distance when he detected the smoke of an unseen campfire. A practice of personal safety caused him to check the impulse to hurry toward the water that his thirsty body cried out for. As he paused, a shot rang out, followed by a discordant cry of pain.

Cautiously, he moved forward, stopping often to listen intently, careful to keep in line with some large rocks a hundred yards away in the direction of the rifle report.

It was with a great sense of relief that he reached the safety of this rocky haven. He dropped to his knees, chest heaving from the exertion. He could hear voices but couldn't make out what they were saying. Venturing to peer from his hiding place, he was surprised to see a campfire so close. Several horses were tethered to some stunted trees, and he could make out the dim outline of a wagon just outside the ring of light.

Three men were standing with their backs to him, hands extended over their heads. Across the fire from them stood a small, boyish figure in baggy, oversized clothes with a hat pulled down close over the eyes. A man was laying prone on the ground, arms outflung.

"You git on them horses and leave outta here, NOW!" the boy yelled in a shrill voice, waving a heavy gun back and forth threateningly.

"Come on, boy, you don't stand a chance agin the three of us," snarled the apparent leader of the group, as they began to spread out.

The rider saw the lad's immediate danger and stepped out into the night, rifle in hand.

"He does now—I've just evened the odds—now do as the boy says—you gents fork your horses and get out of here!" he called out in a strained voice.

The three whirled as one to face their unseen adversary, unsure of what they had heard.

"That's right, you heard me the first time, an' if you didn't, here's something to make a believer out of you," he croaked menacingly, firing off a couple of shots at their feet.

It was ludicrous to see three grown men, pushing and falling over one another, in the mad rush for their horses. To hurry their effort he fired another round over their heads.

"That ought t' do it," he muttered. He stood listening to the fading hoofbeats, then turned his attention back to the camp. The boy stood with the rifle leveled in his direction.

"Please—I need water—"

"Lay down your guns and come into the light with your hands high," was the reply.

"Rowdy, come!"

When the big horse stood by his side the rider slipped the rifle into its scabbard. Removing his gun belt, he hung it over the saddle and walked forward into the light, weaving on his feet.

"Stop right there and take off that hat!" was the command.

The man did as he was told, revealing a shock of sandy-colored hair and strained blue eyes.

"There's water in that spring over there," the boy said, indicating the direction with his gun. "Help yourself, Mister."

Following his horse who had already headed that way, the rider threw himself full length at the water's edge to drink. The cool water tasted sweet. He doused his head and rolled over on his back to lay looking up at the night sky as the unconsciousness of sleep overtook him.

2

$\mathcal{H}$E WAS AWAKENED by someone kicking his boot. The sun was already peeping over the canyon wall. Blinking his eyes, he looked up to see the boy leaning over him.

"Are you all right, Mister?"

He sat up as the boy backed away. "I think so, son." He looked around at the strange surroundings, trying to recall where he was. Rowdy was nearby, munching some grass near the small pool of water. His gear lay near the wagon.

"You were so still I thought you were dead. There's some food keepin' warm on the fire when you're ready."

The man rolled over and looked at his reflection in the water. "No wonder the boy was so scared," he muttered. With his red eyes and unshaven face covered with alkali dust, he looked a fright. Getting to his feet, he stretched to relieve his stiff, sore muscles. Rowdy stood nearby with one of the wagon horses.

"Rowdy, come! Let's make ourselves more presentable."

"I've already fed your horse, Mister."

"Thank you, son, that's mighty kind of you. Rowdy doesn't let many people near him. He must have taken a likin' to you."

"He's a grand horse!" the boy exclaimed, eyes lighting up as he looked at Rowdy.

Taking some toilet articles from his saddlebag, the rider went to the water to wash and shave. He rinsed his sweaty shirt and spread it on a nearby bush to dry, then donned a clean one. All the while, out of the corner of his eye, he noticed the boy, who was sitting by a makeshift tent, watching him with curious eyes. A rifle rested on his knees.

What were these two doing way off out here? Two! He had forgotten the man he had seen stretched out on the ground last night.

"Where's your pa?"

"Sleepin'."

"Kinda late to be sleeping, isn't it?"

"You just got up."

"So I did," said the man, grinning. "Now where is that food?"

He approached the fire casually to find a plate of food laying on a rock. He had not realized how hungry he was.

"There's coffee in the pot."

He poured himself a cup and found a seat. Turning his attention to his plate, he did not look up until it was empty. He laid it aside and sat back to enjoy his coffee.

"You're a good cook, boy, what's your name?"

"I'd be obliged if you told me yours first, Mister."

"Well, sir, seeing you've got the advantage, I'll be obliging. I am Wes Scott from the state of Georgia."

A groan came from within the tent. The boy jumped to his feet and disappeared inside. Wes followed him to stand just outside.

"It's gonna be all right, Pa, just you lay quiet," the boy said, a sob very near the surface. He looked up at Wes. "It's the fever. He's worse!"

"What happened?"

"Those men shot him."

"Let me take a look at the wound. The bullet may still be in there." Wes entered to kneel at the man's side. The boy looked at him in alarm but said nothing as he watched Wes examine his pa with deft fingers.

The bullet had entered the right side but had not come out the back. Turning the man on his side, Wes could feel the hard lump where the lead was. It would be easy to remove.

"We'll have to get that bullet out. You get some hot water while I sterilize my knife. Find something to make clean bandages too."

While the boy scurried off to comply, Wes sharpened his knife on a stone and held it over the fire. The boy's pa was fortunate that the remains of the bullet were so close to the surface.

A few minutes later the job was done, and after cleansing the wound, Wes was ready to put on the strips of clean cloth the boy had brought to him.

"Boy, go look in my saddlebag and get that can of ointment for me, and we'll soon be done."

Applying the salve the boy brought to him, Wes carefully wrapped the shoulder.

"That should do it. Barring any complications, he will heal. You might bathe his face some to keep the fever down. I'll look in on him later. I think I'll take a look around the canyon to see how far those scoundrels went. Keep your gun handy."

Wes backed out of the tiny shelter and strode to where Rowdy stood in the shade. The sun was already burning through his shirt. Throwing the saddle on his mount took only a moment. Then he went to the spring to fill the canteen, taking a long draught himself.

He mounted in a singular movement and turned Rowdy onto the trail left by the three riders. He had gone some distance before he noticed any break in the gait of their broncos. They had walked their mounts for a ways, finally coming to a halt before going on.

Wes had not gone much farther when he saw where they had veered to the right into a boulder-strewn gully to make camp. The ashes were cold, so they had headed out early, probably before daylight. He tracked on for a short distance, then turned Rowdy back to camp. They were out there somewhere, even though he saw no dust trail. No doubt, not more than a day's ride. He would have to be watchful. If he could find a high spot near camp, he could use his spyglass to spot them in the distance.

"Come on, Rowdy, it's time we hustled back to check on those folks."

The chestnut did not check his stride until Wes hauled back on the reins as he neared the camp. He called out to the boy to let him know he was riding in but saw no one. He dismounted and threw the saddle. Rowdy headed for water, and Wes strode over toward the tent. The boy stepped out from the rocks, rifle in hand.

"Did you see sign of them?" he asked, shading his eyes from the sun.

"Nope, but they're out there. You can count on that. I saw where they made camp about three miles out. Made tracks before sunup. Unless there's water on ahead, they'll be back. We'll have to take turns watching. The nights will be the worst—we can't see them at night. But Rowdy will let us know. How's your pa?"

"He hasn't come to yet."

Wes went in to check the unconscious man. The bleeding had stopped, and the wound didn't seem as angry looking.

"He's going to be all right. It'll take some time though. Keep his fever down with those wet compresses."

Wes went outside to stand staring down the trail. A frown wrinkled his good-natured face. This camp location was a good one, with unscalable cliffs at their back. No one could sneak up on them from the rear. He needed a spot with a commanding view. When he turned, the boy was on his knees in the opening of the shelter, looking up at him with solemn eyes.

It was the first time that he had taken the time to look closely at the lad's features. Wide-set hazel eyes, with long golden lashes gave the round, smooth face a girlish appearance. The mouth that had been taut and drawn in the first hours of his appearance was now relaxed in soft curves turning up at the corners.

"What's your name, boy? I can't go on just calling you boy."

"Uh—Lee," came the almost shy answer.

"Well, Lee, I need to find a high spot back up in those rocks so I can keep a lookout with my glass. You can stand watch during the day, and I'll move your pa back in the rocks and leave the camp just as it is. You fix up some food and stash it back there, and I'll fill up vessels of water and carry them up."

"There's a good place not too far. I'll show you."

Wes followed the youngster back through a narrow passageway between the boulders, stooping to get through where they leaned against the wall of the canyon. The path led about 20 yards ending in a small square opening. Spent shells, laying half buried in the rocky soil, gave evidence that others before them had used this spot.

"We'll bring your pa here. You can start bringing up what you'll need while I scout on a little higher up."

Turning to study the seemingly unscalable walls surrounding him, Wes noticed some indentations that had been made in the large rock facing the camp below. By placing his feet in the niches, he was able to pull himself up to the top. His position there gave him a commanding view of the desert below. It was more than he would have hoped for. He gave a grunt of satisfaction and eased himself back to the ground. Even the boy could climb up there with his help.

It took only a few moments to make his way back down the path to the lower camp where he found Lee busy around the fire.

"Cook up enough biscuits for several days," Wes suggested, "we might be up there a spell, depending on how well your pa does."

The boy nodded his head and went on with his work without looking up. Wes paused to watch as the lad shaped the dough into round balls, patted them down, then put them into an iron pan sitting in the coals. He placed a lid on top and put a scoop of hot coals on it.

"Somebody's done a good job of teaching that boy to cook," he murmured to himself.

For the next half hour, Wes busied himself with carrying the things they would need up the trail to their hiding place. This finished, he surveyed his work with satisfaction. Lee's call to come and eat hastened him back to camp.

3

*W*ES KNELT by the still unconscious man. He was of slender stature with a fine, sensitive face and regular features. His dark, graying hair was matted to his head. He looked to be in his early 50s. The hands laying at his side did not bear the callouses of a hardworking man.

"It's just as well that you're still out, fella, cause this is going to hurt some. I just hope it doesn't start the bleeding all over again," Wes spoke softly, lifting the man into his arms.

"Lee, grab those blankets and that tarp and run ahead of me. It'll take me awhile to work my way up there. You can fix a place to lay him down."

The boy swiftly obeyed, stopping only to grab up his rifle before running up the steep trail. Wes followed as quickly as he could, laboring under the heavy load. Breathless and perspiring, he was relieved when he reached the end. Lee had placed the blankets in a sheltered area where the rocks protruded out overhead and stood ready to help him as he lowered his burden to the ground.

The injured man moaned and tried to speak. Kneeling beside him, Lee tenderly stroked his forehead to comfort him. "You'll be fine, Pa, you're getting better."

Wes checked the wound for bleeding. "So far, so good," he said with relief. "There's no more bleeding. He should be coming around soon. You stay here and tend to him, and I'll finish up below."

The sun was low in the west when Wes watered the horses and secured them in full sight of the lookout above. He threw some wood on the fire and watched it until a tiny flame appeared.

Casting a glance around, he was satisfied at his handiwork. From all appearances it would look as if they were fast asleep in their blankets. He filled the last of the canteens and moved on up to join the others. If there was time, he wanted to study the desert once more before it became too dark. It was important to know and identify every crack and crevice, tree and shadow. Any change would serve as a warning and work in their behalf, giving them the edge.

When he stepped into the small clearing, the injured man was looking up at him with questioning eyes. Lee was nowhere to be seen.

"My—boy—where?" he gasped with alarm, trying to sit up.

"Whoa, partner, I wouldn't try to sit up just yet," Wes admonished, kneeling to push the man back. "He's around here somewhere."

"I'm up here, Pa," Lee called from atop the rock. At the same time two legs appeared, feeling for the tiny steps. His descent seemed effortless, and soon he dropped nimbly to the ground.

"Are you all right—boy?" the father whispered weakly, eyes lighting up at the sight of him.

"Yes, Pa, I'm fine! Oh, this is Wes Scott," Lee continued, as his father's eyes focused on Wes with a questioning look.

"He came along just in time to help us."

"Thank God!" Tears glistened in his gray, somber eyes.

"Where—are we?"

"We're up in the rocks above the camp. Mr. Scott thought it wise to move up here 'til you're better. Those men might come back."

"Please—you'll not harm them—"

"Pa! Those men meant to hurt us! They shot you and would have done worse to me! How can you plead for them!"

"Hush, child—let me talk. Mr. Scott, thank you for intervening on our behalf, but I am a man of the cloth and cannot let you hurt these men," he continued in a halting voice.

"Well, the way I see it, sir," Wes began, getting to his feet, "it's either shoot or be shot, and I intend to live as long as I can. What about that fine boy you have? You need to think about what would have taken place if I hadn't come along. It was my horse who led me here."

Picking up a few of the dry sticks he had gathered, Wes built a small, smokeless fire and set the coffeepot on it. He sat down with his back against the rock and stared at the blaze. The boy gave his father a drink from one of the canteens and sank back on the blanket to lay there, gazing up with luminous eyes at Wes, who seemed unaware of their presence.

What was he thinking about? Was it that girl whose picture was in the locket that fell out of the saddlebag when he was looking for the salve? She was young and pretty. Lee could not help but wonder who she was.

The coffee boiled over in the fire, and Lee grinned at Wes's antics as he grabbed the hot handle. He poured himself a cup and sat watching the dying coals. Finally, he set the cup aside and got to his feet. He checked the gun in his holster, whirling the chamber, then picked up his rifle. It was getting late in the day and already the shadows had deepened in their little sanctuary.

"Lee," he called softly, "are you awake?"

"Yes" came the reply.

"I'm going up on the rock. Did you see any sign earlier?"

"Nope."

"Well, I don't look for any action from them until tomorrow. They'll probably move up some tonight, then wait to hit us late in the evening. You get some rest, son," he concluded in a gentler tone. "You've been a real help today."

Wes climbed up to his lookout position and stretched out on his stomach, laying the rifle handy at his side. Extending the small telescoping glass, he studied the desert floor beneath him. It seemed a futile effort, and he was about to give it up when a pinpoint of light appeared, then vanished. He intently watched the spot for what seemed a long time. Perhaps his weary eyes were deceiving him. No, there it was again.

"They're out there all right," he muttered.

He rolled over on his back to look up at the night sky where stars gave off a brilliant light. A cool breeze fanned his cheek as he pondered the situation. There were three of them and only one of him. If he waited for them to come to him, there would be shooting and they might get lucky. That would put these people at greater risk.

Why wait? Why not go to them? To surprise the enemy was always in your favor. They would not be suspecting such an action. He turned to catch another glimpse of the faint gleam in the distance. It was still there. By them moving in that close tonight meant they were planning to try to overpower them in the early hours tomorrow morning.

Seems as if they are going to be there awhile. One thing was sure. He would need to find their camp before they headed out. If he didn't, Lee and his father would be in grave danger.

An uneasy thought pressed into his consciousness. What if it wasn't them? It could even be a decoy, hoping to draw him away or divert his attention from what was close at hand.

Wes lowered his glass to look down at Rowdy. The horse's ears were up and his head was held high, looking out into the darkness.

"Uh huh! Good boy, Rowdy," Wes whispered quietly. His growing admiration for this great horse the colonel had given him as a farewell gift made his heart swell with pride.

It was a good thing he had not moved out into the light of the dying fire. He raised the glass again to peer into the area close around the camp, carefully studying every rock and tree, measuring the density of the shadows surrounding them. Taking another look at Rowdy, Wes saw him lower his head and paw the dirt, then quickly raise it again. A good indication that whoever was out there must be nearby.

Wes reached for his rifle and took a few of the shells from his pocket, laying them on the rock before him. This done, he concentrated his attention on the dim perimeter encircling the animals below. Was there a shadow by that big clump of greasewood that wasn't there before? To get a better look he reached for his glass. Hearing a slight sound behind him, he glanced over his shoulder to see the boy pulling himself up over the edge of the boulder.

"Keep your head down," he warned with a whisper. "I think we have company below. What are you doing up here?"

"I couldn't sleep. I heard you talking to yourself. Pa's sleepin', so I thought I would come up and help you watch for a while. Uh—you don't mind, do you?"

"No, I reckon not. It might be safer for you up here anyway. Did you bring your gun?"

"Yes."

"Good! I think the fireworks will begin here any minute. See that greasewood bush out there to your right toward the spring? Look sharp," Wes continued, "see that dark spot? Watch and see if it moves."

Lee inched forward to get a better view, body tensed, rifle held so not to make a sound against the stony surface. He could see the horses now. Rowdy was standing as if carved in stone, head alert, mane flowing down his neck. Lee thrilled at the sight of him. It was hard to draw his eyes to the bush that Wes had indicated.

"Yes, I see it."

"Can you fire that gun?" Wes asked, looking over at the youngster.

"Yes, Pa taught me. He thought that since I was a—uh—that if something should happen to him and I would be alone—I—I should know," Lee answered, almost inaudibly.

Wes nodded his head but did not reply immediately. Lee remained silent and watchful beside him.

"Ya' better take off your hat, boy, before someone takes a potshot at it."

"No. I won't do that."

"Then you just better keep your head low, or your brains are going to be ventilated. Shhh! Something moved by that big cactus. It's a man getting to his feet. See, there's another by the bush. Where's the other one? There, coming from behind that small mesquite tree. They're coming in, boy, hold your fire until you hear me shoot. If one of them makes it into the wall, I'll have to leave you here and go down to hold him off."

Bright bursts of gunfire suddenly split the night air as the enemy approached what appeared to be a sleeping camp. Wes could hear the bullets as they thudded into the makeshift bodies, accompanied by coarse, gleeful shouts. Rowdy was wild-eyed, straining at his tether. Still, Wes held his fire.

"Haw, haw! We should have made them dance, Gar," chortled one of them as the shooting ceased. "This was too easy!"

"Shaddap, Slinker, 'n build up that fire," ordered Gar, the apparent leader of the group. "We'll look 'round and see if we can find some loot on these gents, maybe some likker. Hustle! Red, you bring in our horses."

"Hey, Boss! Take a look at this hoss! Whoa! Haw, haw! Looks like he's a mean 'un. We'll take that outta 'im! Huh, Gar," Red exclaimed, excitedly.

"Slinker, where are you with that wood? Get it in here so we can see sumpin'!" yelled the burly leader.

"I'm a-comin' . . . hold on!" Slinker called back, his arms laden with sticks.

Wes started moving back to reach the steps. "I reckon it's time. If they start searching those fake bodies, it'll be all day with us. You stay here and cover me. Don't fire and give away your position. If something happens to me, it's up to you. Take care of yourself, boy." With that he was gone.

Lee anxiously watched the men below to see if they were aware of their impending danger. Two of them were standing near the horses and the one called Slinker was coming back toward them. Where was Wes?

4

AT THE BOTTOM OF THE TRAIL Wes paused to listen. Had he made it down before Slinker came back? Should he risk taking a look? They could be facing his way. The colonel's words came back to him. "If you're going to spy on someone, don't do it at eye level." To lessen his chances of being detected, he knelt close to the ground before peeping out. Two of the murderous thieves had their backs to him, watching Rowdy as he reared with front feet pawing the air. The other was approaching the fire to drop his armload of wood.

Their rifles were leaning against a rock, but each wore a gunbelt. This would be his only chance to catch them off guard before they discovered they had been tricked.

Wes stood to his feet and sprang into the open, getting in several strides before the men were aware of his presence. It was Slinker who saw him first and he dropped the wood on the fire, his mouth gaping as if he had seen a ghost. Before he could muster enough voice to cry out a warning, Wes shouted, "Put your hands in the air and turn around!" The two men with their backs toward him stiffened, hands clawing the air. They spun around to face their adversary.

"You!" Gar cried, his surly face working.

"Don't make a move toward those guns, gents, or you'll be packing lead. Now get over here, that's it, stop right there."

"Lee!"

"Right here, Wes."

"Come down here and cover these vermin while I tie them up!"

* * *

Wes stood to his feet and stretched his stiff, weary body. His movement startled an animal at the spring, and he could hear it move away through the brush. In the east was a light glow announcing the dawn of another day. It had been a long night, and he was glad to welcome the coming of day.

His prisoners lay prone in sleep, hands and feet tied. Today he would have to dispose of them. He had no idea where the nearest town was, and besides they didn't have enough food to feed the extra mouths. To keep them around would be a constant threat.

Picking up a bucket, he went to the spring for water. As soon as it was light enough, he would have to scrounge around for fuel for the fire. There was not enough kindling left to last through breakfast.

Rowdy lifted his proud head and whinnied for attention from his master as he returned to set the pail down. Wes went over to him and patted him on the neck. "What is it, Rowdy?" he whispered, so as not to awaken the sleeping captives. "Do you want a drink?" He slipped the knot on the reins and led Rowdy to the spring while the other horses looked on and grew restless.

Leaving the big chestnut to nibble on what few sprigs of green grass remained in the moist soil near the water, Wes headed out to gather what he could find to burn. When he returned to camp, Lee was raking coals together to start a fire.

He dropped his burden beside the boy and stood watching as the lad broke some of the smaller twigs to lay on top, blowing it until a feeble flame appeared, licking hungrily at the tiny bits of wood.

"How's your pa?" queried Wes, brushing himself off.

"Oh, he's a heap better," Lee answered, laying more wood on the fire. He gathered up the makings for biscuits, returning to place them on a nearby rock before continuing. "With some help, he could probably make it down on his own."

A grunt came from one of the prisoners. Wes turned to meet the direct gaze of the one called Gar. Glittering, deep-set eyes expressed cunning and hatred. The swarthy face with its full beard supported a cruel mouth that drew back in a snarl, baring yellowed, tobacco-stained teeth.

"It ain't human to make us sit like this."

"Considering the treatment you were trying to give to us, I'd say we are being very humane, and right now, you'll stay put until I decide what to do with you," Wes responded, turning his back on them. The sleepless night had left him in no mood to be lenient with these unwanted guests.

Lee put on the coffeepot. Soon it was steaming, giving off a wonderful aroma in the cool desert air. Wes poured himself a cup and hunkered down by the fire. He liked this time of day. It always seemed to him that no matter what the troubles of yesterday had been, a new day held forth hope and challenge. He felt a pang of loneliness as he remembered the many times he and the rest of the men in Colonel Stothards' command had shared the predawn hours around the campfire.

A feeling of restlessness swept over him. Getting to his feet, he turned to stare at the desert with unseeing eyes. He wouldn't be here in this wild, forlorn place, away from his friends, if it wasn't for Testa. She was in this desert wilderness somewhere, and he had promised his mother he would find her and bring her home, if it wasn't too late. Twice he had just missed them by a day. They were traveling light, keeping on the move, never staying in one place more than a day or two.

Probably gambling to get enough money to support themselves.

Tessie had always been headstrong, and with him gone so much of the time, it had been increasingly more difficult for their mother to control her. He and his sister were as different as night and day. She took after their father who had been lost at sea. Wes had sandy hair and blue eyes. Tessie had dark eyes set in a piquant face framed with a mass of black hair. Her temperament, so different from his own, was excitable and adventuresome. They had all assumed she would marry Alex Brunner, that nice young man who worked in a print shop. Certainly he was deeply in love with her and was heartbroken when she ran off with that smooth-tongued gambler.

Rowdy clipped off a clump of grass and raised his head to watch his master, then he moved over to nuzzle Wes's hand, as if to comfort him. Lee's call to breakfast broke into his reverie. Leading Rowdy back toward the wagon, Wes left him there. He washed his hands and came to take the steaming plate of biscuits and beans offered him. Lee came to where he sat cross-legged on the ground and filled his cup with coffee before taking up his own plate.

"You make a decent cup of coffee, Lee. Thanks."

When no response came, Wes glanced over at Lee, who seemed to be giving full attention to eating. White flour fingerprints showed on the brim of the battered hat pulled low over the boy's eyes. Under his direct gaze, a wave of crimson spread over the fair face, giving Wes cause to wonder.

"I'll go see if your father can make it down. Those other horses will need to be watered," Wes commented, breaking the awkward silence. He laid his empty plate aside and stood to his feet before continuing. "Stay away from those men, and keep a sharp lookout. There's always a chance for danger near a water hole. I won't be gone long."

Lee's eyes followed the lean, lithe figure of the man as he strode off, spurs jingling. Hurriedly gathering up the soiled plates, Lee went to the spring to wash them, ignoring the pleas of the bound men to come and give them something to eat. When they saw that there was no help forthcoming, they turned to cursing and trying to free themselves. Lee picked up the rifle and pointed it right at Slinker who was scooting over toward Gar.

"Hold it right there! Move away from him!"

"What you aimin' to do about it, boy?" sneered the outlaw.

Red sat quietly, as he had done all morning, like a coiled rattler, just waiting for an opportune time to strike. He appeared to be the youngest of the three, aged beyond his years by the hard life he had chosen.

"I aim to shoot you if you don't move back where you belong right now!" Lee warned, raising his gun to sight down the long barrel. "MOVE!"

"You're kinda cocky, aren't ya, since that feller came along," jeered Slinker, as he moved back to his former position.

Lee continued to keep guard until Wes returned with the wounded man leaning heavily against him.

"Did they give you trouble?" he asked, as he paused to catch his breath.

"Not much," Lee replied. He ran to assist Wes in getting his pa into the wagon bed. After making the injured man as comfortable as possible, Wes turned to give the three would-be assassins a cold, icy stare.

"Well, they'll not be troubling you much longer. Tend to your father and load up the wagon. Be sure to fill everything you have with water. Where are your horses?"

"Those men told Pa they ran off."

"It's an old trick, boy, those animals might stray a little hunting food, but they wouldn't go far from water. No matter, we've got horses enough here."

"You're not takin' our hosses?" hissed Red in disbelief, starting an uproar of threats and cursing.

"Did you feed them?" Wes queried, disregarding the trio glaring at him.

"Didn't get a chance to," Lee answered from the wagon where he was giving his pa food and drink.

"I'll take care of it."

For the next hour, Wes busied himself with feeding the stock, checking each wheel, and building a shelter over the wagon bed to shade Lee's father. This done, he saddled Rowdy and tied him to the back of the wagon.

"Lee, gather up their guns and put them under the seat," Wes instructed, thoughtfully studying the horses before him. Choosing the sturdier two of the three, he led them to the wagon and hitched them up. Then he tied the remaining horse behind with Rowdy.

"Can you drive this outfit, Lee?" Wes asked, as he checked to make sure all was ready.

"I—I think so," was the reply. "I'm not used to those horses."

"Well, you'll be all right if you keep a tight rein and walk them. Climb aboard and hand me one of those pistols and a knife belonging to these gents."

Lee was quick to obey, handing Wes the weapons. "Drive the team out a ways and wait for me. I'll be along shortly," Wes told him.

"You're not—you won't—" Lee's voice faltered.

"I won't do anything I can't live with," Wes answered grimly. "Now head them out! That sun's already getting warm."

He stepped clear and gave the nearest horse a light slap, watching until they were out of range where Lee brought the horses to a halt.

Wes turned his attention to the men laying bound before him. "Spread out more—get a move on," he commanded, leveling the revolver at them. Slinker started scooting over, but Red and Gar only glared insolently at their captor. Wes fired two shots close enough to make them jump. "Move!" he ordered.

This time they were only too glad to comply, moving until Wes ordered them to stop. "That's far enough, boys. Seeing I'm in such a good mood, I'll even leave you a few shots in your gun, and give you a knife. Whoever gets loose first is welcome to them," he concluded, placing them high on a rock.

5

*W*ES FOLLOWED THE WAGON TRACKS over the rough terrain, grinning to himself. There was no honor among thieves, and as he had left them, the three were already glaring distrustfully at one another. All understood that the first one freed would have the upper hand.

Lee was watching for him and beckoned from the wagon. Wes quickened his steps. As he drew nearer, he was struck by the whiteness of the boy's face. Horror-stricken eyes stared at him as he stepped up into the wagon.

"Did they—did you—?"

"Shoot them? No—I just used up a couple of their shots. I didn't want to leave them too much ammunition. Don't worry any more about them."

"I was worried about you," Lee said tremulously, turning his head away.

Wes had no immediate answer for Lee's revealing remark. No one had worried over him for a long time. It had always been Testa. Pulling his hat low on his forehead to shield his eyes from the sun, he took the reins and coaxed the horses into a fast walk. The wagon bumped over the stony ground, jarring its occupants. A rabbit, startled by the noise, dashed off into a clump of creosote bushes, its cottontail a flash of white.

The canyon widened and the obscure trail became less rough. Distant cliffs stood aloof in the shimmering heat waves.

As they moved out into the wide expanse of the desert, Wes could see buzzards circling high overhead. They would soon be feasting on horse meat.

"Where ya' headed?" Wes asked finally, breaking the silence.

"Don't reckon I know. Pa says the Lord will let us know when we get there. Every town we come to, I kinda look it over real good—wondering if it'll be the one."

Lee shifted his position, placing his feet on the front kickboard of the wagon. After studying his scuffed, dusty boots a moment, he added an afterthought, "We may have to go clear to California before we know. I think I'd like that. I want to see the Pacific Ocean. Have you seen it?"

"No, I haven't," mumbled Wes, trying to keep his eyes open. The heat bearing down on his weary body clouded his mind and made his eyes heavy with sleep. If he could just hold on for a couple more hours, maybe he could rest while the boy rustled up something to eat.

"Lee," his father called out weakly.

The boy scrambled over the seat, to kneel by his side. "What is it, Pa?"

"Give me a drink."

Lee found a canteen and held it to his father's lips, noting with relief that his father's face was clammy and wet. The fever was gone. It was warm under the makeshift tent, but the air moving through made it bearable.

"Where are we?"

"I don't know," Lee answered finally, realizing he didn't even know what direction they were traveling, "but we are safe. You must rest now. We'll stop soon, and I'll fix you something to eat."

"Lee, you mustn't let him know that you're a—"

"Sssh!" Lee laid a hand over his father's lips. "He might hear you," he whispered. "Rest!"

He waited until his father was sound asleep again before returning to the seat beside Wes.

"How's he doing?"

"Fever's broke. He's asleep again," Lee replied.

Wes nodded his approval without taking his eyes off the trail ahead. He had slowed the horses to preserve their strength as the desert sun grew hotter. The time dragged by slowly.

The scrubby growth of the canyon had given way to an abundance of green greasewood bushes and stunted mesquite trees, dotted with an occasional paloverde, the Spanish word for green stick. Wes was always intrigued by the sight of the tree with its long, needle-like leaves the same color as the smooth trunk. He had been told they grew slowly, taking hundreds of years to reach 10 inches in circumference. It was different from any tree he had ever seen. Seemingly so fragile, yet it had the tenacity to survive in this arid, rocky soil.

He remembered what an old prospector had told him. "Well, sonny, the desert will either make or break a man or a woman. It will bring out the good or the bad. If you learn to respect it and accept its solitude, the desert will be kind to you and share its secrets."

The dim trail was leading into a narrow, rock-strewn, dry streambed, lined with weather-beaten cottonwoods. Wes brought the wagon to a stop under one of them, grateful for the shade.

"We'll stop here a spell," Wes said, securing the reins. "There's plenty of wood for cooking."

Stepping down, he stretched wearily and turned to help Lee down, but the boy jumped nimbly to the ground, ignoring Wes's outstretched hand. Together, they gathered enough wood for a fire, and while Lee made preparations to cook, Wes walked up on the trail a little way. It wound along the bank for about a half mile, then vanished over a low rise ahead.

Retracing his steps, he found Lee busy at the fire. His father was sitting, propped up against the trunk of the big cottonwood, pale but alert.

"Hello! It's good to see you up and around, sir. After we eat, I'll take a look at that wound. It may need a new dressing."

"Lee says you are Wes Scott from Georgia?"

"Savannah, sir, my father was a sea captain, and I served in the war under Colonel Stothard."

The man nodded, scrutinizing Wes from head to toe, taking in the tanned, boyish face and steady blue eyes. He liked what he saw. However, in light of what had happened to them, one must be careful, especially for Lee's sake.

"My d—uh—Lee and I want to thank you for the help you have given to us. It troubles me deeply to think about what would have happened to us both, had you not come when you did. Certainly God sent you to us."

Out of the corner of his eye, Wes saw Lee's head snap up as he gave his father a warning glance.

"Well, I don't know about that," Wes replied, with a grin. "I was pretty bad off myself. I think Rowdy would have smelled the water. He knew you were there first." He shifted his gunbelt and sat crosslegged on the ground. "You said you were a preacher?"

"Yes. I am Hiram J. Webster. Until a year ago, I was circuit-riding pastor of five churches near Fort Smith, Ark." A look of sadness came over Webster's face, and he stared off in space.

"What are you and your son doing out here traveling alone?" Wes urged when it seemed no further information was forthcoming. "Didn't you consider the danger involved in a venture such as this?"

The preacher's eyes returned to Wes, who was taken aback at the pain he saw in them. "No, I guess I didn't," Webster replied finally, with a strained voice. "After my—my wife died, I—I couldn't think straight—I lost everything—my faith, my confidence, and then my parish. I didn't want to live. If it hadn't been for my—for Lee, I would have ended it all."

Further conversation ended as Lee brought each of them a plate of food. After pouring them coffee, he took a plate and came to sit by his father. Each gave full attention to eating. When Wes was finished, he got up to attend to the horses. Then, finding a level place in the shade, he removed his gunbelt and stretched out on his back, holding his gun in his hand.

"Lee, keep a sharp lookout and wake me in a little while. Don't touch me, just say my name. We'll need to move on, try to find water if we can," he mumbled as he fell asleep.

It seemed he had just closed his eyes when he heard Lee's call. Although the sun was already slanting toward the west, the heat was relentless. Wes got to his feet. While he buckled on his gun, he looked the camp over. Everything had been carefully put away. He took his seat beside Lee and turned the horses into the trail.

"I see your father is asleep. I'll have to take a look at his wound later." Lee nodded in agreement as Wes went on. "It's hard to say where this trail will lead us, or who used it. But if we're lucky, it might lead into a better one, maybe to a ranch or homestead."

They reached the top of the small grade to be greeted with more of the same sunbaked expanse. The faint track led more to the west now, toward a high butte rising up from the desert floor. To the north, the mountains Wes had observed for most of the day appeared just as far away, mysterious in their dark, brooding, purple hues. The long months on the trail had taught him that distance was deceiving here in the West.

It had been two long, torturous days of travel in the heat for both man and beast. Twice the wagon had thrown a wheel, which was a test of strength for Wes, along with Lee's help, to repair and plop back in place. The nights had seemed too short and the days too long. The dim trail they had started out on ended at an old adobe shack that had long been abandoned. The spring nearby, which had once sustained life, was dried up.

Wes turned back to where Lee and his father waited in the wagon, trying not to let them see his concern. The rivers they had crossed had been dry, the sand molded in flowing designs from water long evaporated by the sun's rays. The meager supply of water they had left was dwindling, even though they had been sparing with it. The horses had already begun to show the effects of the strain. Even Rowdy showed little spirit as he stood listless in the hot sun, his head down.

Scanning the horizon to the west, Wes saw little to give much hope. Ahead of them lay a low range of mountains. To the southwest the open desert. Off to the northwest, cumulus clouds were billowing high in the clear, blue atmosphere.

Avoiding Lee's questioning eyes, he climbed back to his seat and took up the reins. At his urging, the tired horses moved forward, resuming their slow pace. He decided to head toward the low range of mountains in the hope there was a spring there, then skirt them to the south, where they might pick up a main trail leading into a town or even Fort Bowie, which was located somewhere in the southeast Arizona Territory.

The sun was well in the west when they came to the river. Wes brought the horses to a halt, keeping a tight hold on the reins. It was dry except for a tiny stream meandering in the middle. The clouds that had been friendly white puffs in the sky had taken on an ominous look, broken by streaks of lightning. The wind had picked up, and Wes could see a clay-colored pall off in the distance. Dark sheets of rain draped from the clouds, changing shapes with the intensity of the storm.

His mind went back to his conversation with the old prospector at Santa Fe and this phenomena of the desert he had so vividly described. "When you see that comin', sonny, take cover and cover your head. It'll choke you sure enough, and iffen it's bad 'nuff, it'll bury ya. An' don't ya go venturin' inta any of them washes when it's a-rainin' upstream. That water can come down them dry streambeds like a wall, an' ya cain't outrun it."

Wes looked around him for shelter, but there was none. The desert plants were mostly creosote bushes, greasewood, and a few mesquite trees. The horses had grown restless with the smell of water so near and were straining in their harnesses to go forward. It was all he could do to hold them in check.

"Lee, come up here," Wes called to the boy, who had taken refuge from the sun under the makeshift tent with his father.

When Lee had scrambled to the front to look quizzically up at him, Wes pointed to the sky.

"Take a look at that. I think we are in for quite a blow. Looks like a sandstorm coming this way. We need shelter. Start securing things, and get something to cover up with. We'll have to unhitch the horses and turn the wagon over for shelter."

Lee stared in fascination at the approaching storm, then disappeared to unload things and cover them with the tarpaulin, laying stones on the edges, to protect them from the wind and rain. Webster awakened from his stupor to help Lee as much as he could, then came to where he could look out.

"You'll have to climb down, sir," Wes shouted above the wind as he fought to control the horses, and slip them from their harness. Once they were free, he tied them to a mesquite tree nearby and ran to take care of Rowdy.

"Come on, boy, this is gonna be something new to the both of us."

The wind was blowing harder, and the eerie color of the sky was making everything appear in a different light as the red wall of the storm advanced.

"We'll have to hurry," Wes called to the others standing outside the wagon. "We need to turn the wagon over on its side. I'll need your help! Ready! Heave!"

The wagon paused, then gave way to lay with its wheels up. Wes propped up one side with the shovels and hurried Lee and his father under the leeward part, crawling in beside them.

"Cover your heads loosely, leave space to breath," he instructed them above the roar. Taking his kerchief from around his neck, he tied it over his nostrils, turned up his collar, and pulled his hat down low on his forehead.

The storm hit with a ferocity that shook the wagon over them. Choking dust swirled in upon the three of them huddled together, as the wind howled overhead. Streams of sand blew in around them with a hissing sound. A brilliant burst of lightning followed quickly by a deafening clap of thunder caused Lee to cry out and seek shelter in his father's arms. The heat and the swirling dust formed a vacuum that stifled them and stung their eyes.

After what seemed like an eternity, large spattering drops of rain turned into a roar as hail beat down upon them, bringing welcomed relief. Wes removed his scarf and peered out to see how the horses were faring. Outside of prancing around because of the stinging effect of the icy missiles hitting them, they seemed all right.

When the worst of the storm had dwindled to a distant rumble, Wes moved out in the lessening rain to tend to the animals. The wind had stopped and the desert air was cool and refreshing, with the smell of sage. As he walked, his boots crunched in the hailstones covering the ground. Off to the west, the sky had brightened somewhat, promising the end of the rain.

Lee followed suit, helping Mr. Webster to a standing position, where they proceeded to shake the dust from their clothes. When Wes returned with the horses the boy had his pale face turned up to the cool rain.

"Feels kinda good after all that heat and dust, doesn't it, son?" Wes commented, grinning at Lee.

6

*I*T HAD NOT TAKEN LONG to reload their possessions and hitch up the horses. About a hundred yards downriver, Wes had found a lower bank where, with a little shoveling, they could make it across. When all was ready, he left Lee and his father in charge of the wagon, mounted Rowdy, then took up the reins of the extra horse. He paused, listening to the quiet sound of the water. Other than a light increase in the flow, it appeared unaffected by the storm.

"What are we waiting for?" Webster asked impatiently, breaking the silence. "Don't you think we ought to cross while there's still light?"

"Well, I'm not sure," Wes replied, thoughtfully, studying the peaceful flow of the water. "I don't want to take unnecessary risks."

"Risks!" Webster echoed with more spirit. "I can't see where there would be any problems crossing that small stream of water!"

"It's not that stream of water I'm worried about, sir. There could be quicksand or a surge of water from upstream."

"But, that storm is long gone," Webster argued, looking up at the clearing sky. "The least we could do is make it across before dark, or we may have more water to contend with by morning. Come on, Lee, get those horses moving. I say we better cross."

Lee hesitated, looking at Wes, but Webster yelled at the horses, starting them down the embankment.

"Wait!" shouted Wes, leaning out to grab the harness of the nearest horse. But the team had lunged forward too fast for him. Once committed, he rode Rowdy up alongside.

"I'll ride on ahead and check the depth," he called out. Lee nodded grimly in acknowledgment, holding tightly to the reins.

Rowdy stepped out in the lead, hoofs sinking deep in the sandy soil.

"Keep those horses moving so the wagon doesn't get stuck in this sand," Wes instructed. "I'll take this animal over and tie him up, then come back to help you. Hold steady!"

He was pleased to find that the water was no deeper than the belly of the big thoroughbred, who made the crossing easily, pulling the shorter mount along with him up the bank. Wes secured the spare horse and turned back to help with the team just entering the water. Lee's high-pitched voice called them into action as the wagon bumped along over submerged rocks, water coming to the floorboards.

Wes rode out to where he could grab the harness of the nearest horse and urged them forward, suddenly conscious of a subdued rumble that caused his heart to freeze.

"Lee, hurry! There's no time to waste! Hear that sound? We've got to get out of here! Hi yah!" he yelled, hitting the horse with his hat.

The team gave a great lurch forward, as if sensing the danger coming toward them. They were soon free of the water, their hooves digging deep into the sand of the opposite shore. Could they make it up the bank in time? The rumble had given way to a roar.

"Wes, look!" Lee screamed.

Wes felt the blood leave his face as he turned to see a great wall of water in the distance surging toward them. He tossed his rope to Webster, who sat whitefaced beside Lee.

"Tie that to the wagon! Hurry! That's it! Good!"

Wes quickly tied the other end to the pommel of his saddle and called to the big horse. Rowdy leaped forward, pulling the others along. There were only moments left for them to make it to safety. With one last lunge, the horses, eyes rolling in fear, cleared the bank. The wagon careened from one side to the other, upsetting its occupants. Mr. Webster fell over backward into the floor, but Lee was thrown into the riverbed.

"Lee!" Wes shouted, whirling Rowdy around. "Run for it!"

He jumped from his horse and ran to the boy's side. Lee was laying facedown, unconscious. The raging water, pushing its tangled mass of trees and debris, was scarcely a hundred yards away. Wes scooped the boy up in his arms, taking no notice of the hat that had fallen to the ground, releasing a tangled mass of long, golden hair.

With great, leaping strides, Wes made it to safety with little time to spare. He turned to watch the churning, turbulent wall of muddy water as it sped by with a deafening roar, scouring the banks that caved in under the force of the flood. When it reached the bend just below them, the resistance of the curve caused the surging bulk to pile up, flinging logs into the air like straws, sending a great, crashing wave spilling out into the surrounding desert. In all his years around the water, Wes had never seen such a devastating force. The river, which had been so accessible, was now filled to the brink with what looked like liquid mud, writhing and twisting a serpentine course across the desert.

A moan brought him back to the realization that he was still holding Lee in his arms. There was a swollen place on the left temple, along with scratches matted with sand on the cheek. Wes lowered him to the ground, checking to see if there were any broken bones. In astonishment, he jerked his hand away.

"Well, I'll be—you're a GIRL!" he exclaimed in amazement.

He got shakily to his feet and stood, taking in the slender form crowned with golden hair. That explained the long lashes and fair skin, the slender, adept fingers. He swore an oath under his breath as he thought of the danger she was in at the mercy of those outlaws, and the heavy tasks he had allowed, thinking she was a boy. He turned away, disgusted with himself at his lack of intuity.

It was then that he remembered Webster. He went to find him laying in the wagon floor, his face twisted in pain.

"I don't think I've broken anything, just wrenched my shoulder. Where's Lee? Is sh . . . is he all right?"

"Lee's safe. Had a bad bump on the head though. I need to see about him," Wes answered, not giving himself away.

Turning away, he removed his neckerchief, wet it, and knelt to bathe the dirt from Lee's face with a trembling hand. She stirred and moaned again.

"It's all right, Lee, you're safe," Wes choked out, his voice sounding queer in his ears.

Her eyelids fluttered, then opened to reveal hazel eyes glazed with pain. She reached a hand to her temple to feel the swollen knot there. Her questioning gaze came to focus on the scarf, before moving up to his face.

"You were thrown from the wagon and hit your head," Wes explained. "You'll probably have a headache for a while, but that bruise will take a little longer to go away."

He resisted the urge to help her as she struggled to sit up. Long tresses of hair fell around her shoulders, and she gave him a deep, shy glance before looking away. A blush replaced the pallor in her face.

"Now, you know that I'm a—not a boy," she finished finally, in an inaudible voice, stripped of all pretense.

"Yes, I know—and you're safe with me. I have a sister."

"Lee! Are you all right?"

It was her father coming toward them, holding his injured shoulder. Alarmed at the sight of the bruises on her face, he fell on his knees beside her. "Lee, tell me you're all right. Oh, this is all my fault! I should have listened to reason! I lost your mother—and now I almost lost you! How can you forgive me?

Dragging you out in this terrible place, and now this!" His voice broke, and he buried his face in his hands, sobbing, a weakened, broken man.

"Pa, don't take on so! You didn't know! I've just got a bump on my head," she replied in a soothing voice, trying to calm him. Her eyes implored Wes for help. "Come, we'll go back to the wagon, and I will fix a sling for your arm."

"We'll not go any further today," Wes decided, assisting them to their feet. "Lee, why don't you lie down for a while? You've had a pretty hard knock." He led them over to the wagon and helped them in. "If you need anything, call."

Wes used the last hours of daylight to feed and water the stock, lingering long enough to brush Rowdy down, before tackling the task of finding wood for a fire. In all that time, neither Lee nor her father had ventured from their quarters. His mind was relieved when he checked to find them sound asleep.

Weary and hot, he sat down to rest, leaning against his saddle. The sunset had faded into a faint glow in the west, replaced by growing shades of darkness. Overhead, the stars stretched across the sky in a brilliant myriad of light. The brief relief from the heat brought by the storm was gone, and a warmth radiated from the baked earth, not yet cooled with the coming of night. The evening was sultry and hot.

Wes pushed his hat back from his forehead and brushed aside the damp hair. A gnawing pang in his stomach reminded him that he had not eaten for a long time. Since the food was stored in the wagon where he could not get to it for fear of waking its occupants, there was nothing to do but wait.

He pulled his saddlebags to him. Maybe, just maybe, there was a piece of dried jerky left. Searching through the contents, he was disappointed to find nothing to stem his hunger. "Well, I've done without food before," he muttered, taking a drink from his canteen to fill the emptiness.

As was his custom, he sat very still listening to every sound in the desert night, identifying its source. A covey of quail had gone to roost in a nearby mesquite tree, clucking in contented confusion. Out along the river, a coyote gave off its mournful cry, to be answered by a distant chorus, sending a chill up his back. It was a sound one would have to get used to, he mused.

His thoughts turned to the sleeping girl above his head. The situation had grown even more perilous than they seemed to realize. What would have become of them if he had not happened upon them when he did? No doubt they would have perished in the desert, as so many trusting souls before them, robbed and murdered by unscrupulous thieves or renegade Indians roving the area, never to be heard of again. Lee would have suffered a worse fate. A tremendous weight settled in to rest upon him as he contemplated what lay ahead. Now, two women's welfare depended on his ability to help them, he admitted grimly. One was the victim of her own fiery rebellious nature, the other, of circumstances involving loyalty to her father.

Hiram Webster, whatever he might have been as a preacher and pastor, was weakened by depression and self-pity, making him irrational and indecisive. It appeared he cared deeply for his daughter, but he was so obsessed by his own search for escape from the past that he seemed unaware of the dangers to which they were exposed.

It was all right to believe God would help in time of trouble, Wes supposed. His mother was a firm believer in what she called God's intervention. That worked fine until it was something Wes didn't want to do. Then, with a gleam in her eye, she would firmly say, "God helps those who help themselves." He knew he had better be helping himself, pronto, Wes remembered with a smile.

Living within the sheltered realm of the church, Webster probably had not come in contact with the brutal passions and depravity so evident in frontier life. Wes suspected that Lee's mother had been the real strength behind the man—a quality that was profoundly evident in her daughter.

A muffled sound caught his attention, breaking off his thoughts. Pulling his gun, Wes leaned forward, a dark tense figure, listening intently. There it was again. In the dim light of the stars, he could see Rowdy, looking off in the darkness. Something or someone was out there. He was glad he had obeyed his instinct to not build a fire, for it would have been a beacon to hostile eyes in this flat country.

Recalling the stories he had heard in Santa Fe about marauding Indians who had escaped the reservation and were now terrorizing the southwest, Wes felt his heart skip a beat. What could one man do against these fierce warriors? He got slowly to his feet and stepped back until he felt the sideboards of the wagon pressing into his back. He peered into the night, straining his eyes to catch any movement. His ears picked up a soft thud, this time nearer. Whatever or whoever it was would move then pause before coming on. He noted that Rowdy was much like he was, showing no agitation, only curiosity. The big horse's action caused him to wonder. Could it be another horse?

A dark blot moved in from the dark, taking a form that Wes recognized. The riderless bronc, a pinto, came to a halt near the other animals, head drooping. Suspecting a trick, Wes waited a few moments before moving cautiously among the horses, which had grown restless and wary. He reached for the reins and pulled the tired mount to him.

In the faint light he recognized the saddle and blanket, both army conscript. He ran his hand over the outfit seeking for further identification, but found none. He noted the animal had been ridden hard. It was when he patted the pinto on the neck, that his hand came in contact with a sticky substance. His flesh crawled as he recognized the smell of human blood. It was still fresh! That meant that the rider of this horse was nearby.

Wes dropped the reins and stood in deep thought. Could this have happened in the near vicinity? This would explain the fresh blood. Hardly. He would have heard the shots or cries. He checked the stirrups and found dried blood on the straps. To someone who could read signs, this spoke clearly.

The rider had fallen from his horse during the attack, then managed to get back on his mount, hoping it would take him to safety.

Wes recalled the thud he had detected earlier. After returning to pick up his rifle, he retraced his steps to follow the trail of the pinto. He bent to study the hoofprints, surprised that they had been made by an unshod horse. The army always shoed its mounts. This could be an Indian pony.

Wes hesitated, trying to sort out the facts in his mind, calculating the risks. From his limited knowledge of Indian warfare, he knew they rarely attacked at night. Warily, he edged forward, staying close to the ground, stopping often to listen.

The slumbering occupants of the unprotected wagon were very much in his thoughts, and he was just about to turn back when he spied what looked like a body on the ground ahead. Approaching carefully, he found the person unconscious, with a broken arrow protruding through the chest.

Wes turned the body over and found himself looking into the dark, passive face of an Indian. Long, black hair was braided on each side, held back by a beaded headband. A low, guttural groan came from lips that bore a bloody froth. "You're still alive," Wes muttered out loud, "but you won't be long if I don't get that arrow out of you."

He picked up the limp body of the injured man and packed him back to camp, where he placed him on his side, propping his head against the saddle. On closer examination, it appeared that the shaft had not hit a vital part. To get the arrow out he would have to push it on through. Grimly, he went about the task, and when he had finished, he found himself perspiring freely. He cleansed the wound and applied the salve he always carried with him, then replaced the man's shirt.

"Now, only time will tell whether you make it or not. I've done all I can for you, fella."

As he stood there, thoughtfully staring down at the stoic, noble features of the man, he searched his mind for what limited knowledge he had concerning this native race of people.

Feared by most whites, the name had become synonymous with massacre, scalping, and terror. He had read many graphic reports of attacks made on the pioneers pushing westward. However, he had long suspected that the Indian people, who were pushed farther and farther west by the settlers taking over their homeland, feared the intrusion of the white man more.

Fierce as these warriors were, they could not stop the white man, who came in increasing numbers with dreams of becoming rich. The red man saw his own demise in the diminishing herds of buffalo and other wild game, slaughtered for skins, sport, and a haunch of meat for the travelers of the plains. Wes had seen many of their bones bleaching in the sun.

Now, a broken people, forced to live on reservations where they faced deprivation and starvation, they were no longer allowed to roam free on the land that had been theirs for so long. Not all had succumbed to reservation life, however, for there were still bands of marauding Indians led by Mangas Coloradas and Geronimo, riding down upon unsuspecting settlers, bringing horrible death and destruction.

This man had been shot by one of his own race. What tribe he belonged to, Wes could not tell. He was dressed in buckskin pants and an old linsey shirt. A pair of worn moccasins covered his feet. Around his waist was a belt with a beaded sheath out of which protruded the worn handle of a long knife.

Wes took a saddle blanket, rolled it up, and slipped it under the man's head, replacing the hard saddle. He straightened up and peered into the darkness around him. Where had the Indian been when he was attacked? Had he been followed? The pinto had shown signs of being ridden hard but was not lathered up when he came into their camp. Probably had come some distance, no doubt, had headed for the river in search of water, and had picked up the scent of the horses.

7

THE PIERCING NOTE OF A DESERT BIRD awakened Lee at first light. Stiff, sore muscles protested as she sat up. Her head pounded from the blow she had received in the fall. Raising the edge of the canvas, she peeped out. Wes had his back to her, building a fire. Pulling on her boots was no small task, but she managed without waking her father.

Slipping over the back of the wagon, Lee lowered herself to the ground and stood there, uncertain of what to do. Now that he knew she was a girl, it would make a difference. It always did. Men wouldn't let her do anything anymore. Well she would show him. She smoothed her hair and flung it defiantly over her shoulders. Her hat was nowhere to be seen. With chin held high to hide the sudden shyness she felt, Lee walked to where Wes knelt by the fire.

"Morning, Wes, what can I do to help?"

"Well, you can get the makings for breakfast from the wagon and put some coffee on, while I go see how my patient is," he replied, nodding toward the inert figure on the ground.

"Who is it?" Lee questioned, staring wide eyed at the dark features.

"It's an Indian. He was wounded and his horse brought him into our camp half dead. I did what I could. Poor fella may not make it. He was shot by one of his own race. I took the arrow out of him and patched him up. He hasn't moved, so I don't know whether he's still alive or not."

Wes stood to his feet, wiping his hands on his trousers. He removed his hat to wearily push a shock of sandy-colored hair from his forehead, giving her a tired smile.

Lee was shocked to see how haggard he looked. "You— you haven't slept all night! Wes, were we in danger?"

"More so, now that it's daylight. Indians don't like to fight at night. We're out here in the open where we can be easily spotted if there are any in the area." He paused, eyes scouring the desert around them. "Keep that fire as low as possible. I built it under this mesquite to spread what little smoke there is. We need to eat and get moving. If he's still alive, we'll have to take him with us," Wes concluded, nodding toward the injured man.

Lee hurried to the wagon, surprised to have Wes follow her. "To avoid detection, move slowly and don't make any noise. Wake your pa. He can help stand watch. Tell him what I told you." His eyes studied hers for a moment, then he turned away, unaware of the havoc he had wrought in her heart.

Lee called softly to her father, giving him instructions while she gathered up articles to prepare a hurried meal. Soon there was coffee. Wes came to get a cup, kneeling on one knee while he drank, his rifle ready. "He's still alive," he said quietly. Lee filled a plate with biscuits and beans, handing it to him. Both ate in silence, sitting cross-legged on the ground by the dying fire.

"I can't find my hat," she said presently, laying her plate aside.

"It was lost in the river, I didn't have time to get it. You'll have to cover up that yellow hair, though. If an Indian catches sight of that, we'll all be lost." Wes spoke in a matter-of-fact tone, but his remark brought a blaze of color to her face.

He finished his meal, then went to relieve Hiram Webster and tend to the horses. While her father ate, Lee cleaned up the utensils and packed them away. No one spoke a word as they moved about their tasks. Her father seemed to be in a somber mood, eyes following her as she moved about. Lee flashed him an encouraging smile that brought only a thoughtful look in response. She noted his arm was no longer in the sling.

Lee felt her heart swell in sympathy for him. The events of the past week had overwhelmed him, causing him once again to doubt himself, threatening the return of depression. His superficial wounds had healed and strength was returning. But the deeper wounds—her mother's untimely death, the loss of his parish, and his own self-confidence—were slower to mend.

Lee remembered the day she had answered the door to find the leaders of the church standing there, tight-lipped and resolute, asking to see her father. When Hiram Webster had stepped to the door, his face turned white with shock as they thrust a letter into his hand, demanding his resignation.

The following weeks were a blur as they were forced to dispose of all they possessed except what they could carry in the wagon. It had been hard on her father to see the things that were her mother's carried from the house. But, once on the way, his spirit had lifted and he seemed more like himself. In fact, they had enjoyed the long rides together and the evenings around the camp fire, until those three ruffians had ridden in. It was a good thing she had dressed in some of her father's old clothes and hat to travel in. They all took her for a boy, which saved her from—Wes interrupted her thoughts as he came to where she stood waiting. He motioned for her father to join them before speaking.

"I've hitched up the horses in case we have to make a run for it. But I've been studying our situation, and I think we should stay here until dark and then move out. If there are Indians out there, and we have good reason to believe there are, and we leave now, they'll see our dust or come across our trail. We'd stand little chance against them out in the open. By staying quiet here among these mesquite trees, they might not see us unless they rode right up on us." His serious blue eyes looked from one to the other, waiting for them to speak.

Lee glanced at her father, who nodded his agreement with the plan. "Whatever you think is best, Mr. Scott. Tell us what we can do to help," he said meekly.

"Good! Let's bring that man over here in the shade, then you and Lee stand watch while I get some sleep. Don't move around much. Indians have sharp eyes. If you see anything, call me fast." With that accomplished, Wes unrolled his bed under the wagon, laid his rifle close by, and, holding his revolver in his hand, stretched out to fall asleep instantly.

The hours dragged by for Lee as she watched from her seat in a tree. The late afternoon sun burned in the sky, parching the earth. From where she sat, she could see a lizard on a limb of the tree, watching her with a bright little eye. Its gaze shifted as a tiny bug crawled unsuspectingly toward its doom. Only when a long crimson tongue lapped up its victim did she shift her attention back to the horizons around her, looking carefully for any movement.

Glancing toward her father, she found he had fallen asleep, head sagging heavily upon his chest. Wes had not moved. His hat had slipped back, revealing his ruggedly handsome face. She was well aware of the many times her eyes had sought him out during the long hours of watching. An act she had mentally scolded herself for but found she was unable to keep from doing.

Tearing her eyes away once again, she searched the far reaches around them. There! Off toward the mountain! Was that a dust devil or riders? If only she had Wes's glass. It was probably in his saddlebag. Dropping quickly to the ground, she found it and returned to her seat. It took a moment to locate the area where she saw the dust. Her breath caught in her throat. There were riders headed their direction. She left the tree and crawled to where Wes was sleeping. Timidly she touched his sleeve, but she shrank back in horror, not prepared for his reaction, as he jerked suddenly to a kneeling position, gun leveled in her face.

Terror-stricken, Lee stared wide-eyed into the barrel of the weapon. Instinctively, her hands reached out as a shield for the expected bullet. The color fled from her face, leaving it white; a cry escaped from her lips.

As his sleep-clouded gaze came to focus on her, a pallor replaced the tan in his face. "Great heavens, girl! I could have shot you!" he cried hoarsely, his chest heaving. "I told you to call me! All you had to do was say my name."

Wes released the hammer, jammed the revolver into its holster, and grabbed her trembling hands. "Lee, I'm sorry. I didn't mean to scare you. It's just that you startled me." He pulled her to his shoulder, holding her close to quiet her fear. An errant strand of golden hair brushed across his lips. "What was it you wanted?" he asked in a choked voice.

Lee drew away, remembering the horsemen she had seen. "Riders! I—I saw riders over toward the mountain," she gasped, striving for composure. Retrieving the telescope she had dropped, she handed it to him. "Here's your glass."

Wes jumped to his feet and squinted through the scope.

"It's riders, all right. They've stopped—seem to be looking for tracks. They may be trailing that pinto. Wait! That looks like a group of cavalrymen. Yes! I can see the standard!" he confirmed, excitement mounting in his voice. "There! They've mounted up and are heading this way." He lowered the glass. "Lee, we must not be too far from Fort Bowie. You and your father will be safe there."

Lee's heart sank and she turned her head away to hide her disappointment at his last remark. He would be glad to unburden himself from the responsibility of caring for them. She had hoped—what had she hoped? She suppressed the thought. Not yet 20, she had never been interested in the men who had been attracted to her. Now she found herself attracted to this man who had come into her life quite by chance. Had he held her in his arms one moment longer, she may have betrayed her feelings.

Wes was still watching the progress of the troops and did not notice that she slipped quietly away to her father's side.

"Father, wake up," she urged, shaking him gently. "Wes says there are troops coming. They'll see us to safety."

Hiram Webster scurried to his feet, brushing the dust from his clothes. Facing the direction Lee indicated, his face brightened. "The Lord still cares about us, Lee; the Lord still cares. He hath delivered us!" He drew her closer before continuing. "Frankly, I'll be glad to leave the presence of that gunfighter. I've seen the way you look at him, and I will not tolerate you getting involved with a killer of men. You know what the Bible says, 'They that take the sword . . .'"

"I know, Father, 'will die with the sword.' This man saved our lives. Be realistic. You would be dead now, and I would be worse than dead. You said God sent him to us," she interrupted, speaking in a tone he had never heard her use before.

"Lee, what has gotten into you?" he gasped, taken aback.

Her reply was held in check by the arrival of the troops. Wes had walked out a little way to talk with them. Lee couldn't hear what they were saying, but by the gestures being made, she understood their plight was being discussed.

Presently, with conversation ended, the detachment of men dismounted. Leading their horses, they followed Wes into camp. It did not go unnoticed by Lee that they positioned themselves in a protective circle around the horses, while Wes and a couple of the men walked on to where she and her father waited.

She avoided looking at Wes, keeping her eyes on the man in uniform by his side. Amused but friendly dark eyes took in her shabby appearance. For the first time, Lee realized how she must look in the baggy shirt and coat and rolled up pants that belonged to her father. Vanity came to her rescue. She removed the scarf from her head, permitting the shining crown of hair to fall about her shoulders.

"Lieutenant, this is Rev. Hiram Webster, and his daughter, Lee," Wes was saying.

"Noah Berry at your service, sir," said the lieutenant, touching the brim of his hat. "You too, miss." A broad smile broke the somberness of his tanned face as he bowed slightly.

Lee acknowledged his greeting, liking what she saw in his courtly demeanor. She judged him to be in his early 40s, black hair graying a little at the temples. A short-clipped moustache gave him a distinguished look. He was not as tall as Wes, bearing the same lithe frame of one used to many hours in the saddle.

"Thank you, Lieutenant. My daughter and I will be grateful for your help," Hiram Webster responded, extending his hand.

"Pelo de oro," came a low, gutteral voice.

All turned to see the wounded Indian, staring up at Lee.

"Hello, Joe," Lieutenant Berry said cheerfully. "I see you're going to make it after all."

"Pelo de oro," Joe repeated.

"What is he saying?" Lee asked, curiously.

"'Golden hair.' He's fascinated by your hair," answered the lieutenant. "And I must say, I don't blame him."

"Mr. Scott told me of your intentions to ride out of here tonight," he continued, addressing her father. "It's not a bad idea. This is Apache territory and every minute we stay here, we face danger of attack. It's a full day of hard riding to the fort. For your safety, it's best we move out at dusk."

He turned away to command his men. "Sergeant, assign someone to take care of this wounded man, and post your men. Tell them to keep alert. We'll leave at last light."

Wes hesitated, as if wanting to say something to Lee, but she swept silently by him and went to the wagon, leaving him with her father. He was puzzled by her action but felt perhaps she was intimidated by all the men ogling her.

Instead he asked, "Webster, do you feel strong enough to handle the wagon?"

"I—I think so," was the reply.

"Good! I'll ride alongside. If you get tired, I'll relieve you." Wes left him then and walked to the wagon for a last-minute check. Making sure that everything on the outside was secure, he walked to the back. There was no sound from within.

"Lee," he called softly, sure that she would not be asleep. When no answer came, he called again. "Lee, I need to talk to you." He felt rather than saw her presence in the deepening gloom. "Lee, I apologize for being so bold as to hold you in my arms like I did. I did not mean to take advantage of you. It's just that you were so scared—and—and beautiful, that I—I lost my head. I guess, what I'm trying to say is, I didn't mean to upset you."

Lee came closer. Wes could see her white face with dark luminous eyes looking out at him.

"Sssh, Father may hear you. It's all right, Wes, I understand," she replied, with constraint.

"Good!" He gave a sigh of relief. "We may have a pretty rough ride ahead. Your father will handle the team for a while and I'll ride Rowdy beside you." Out of the corner of his eye he could see Hiram Webster coming toward them. "If anything should happen to me, take Rowdy—he can outride any Indian pony alive. Just yell in his ear and give him his head."

Lee was so affected by his speech that she could only nod her head. Wes paused, waiting for her to speak, but when she did not respond, he started to move away. Hiram Webster had stopped to talk with the corporal who had called to him.

"Wes, wait," she exclaimed, finding her voice with great effort. "You—you would give Rowdy to me? You can't do that! I know how much you love him!"

"You don't understand—I am saying, if I am killed, get on Rowdy and ride like the wind. He'll save you."

"But what about Father?"

"If I am killed, he'll not be able to save you. These men will die trying to save you, but they'll have their work cut out for them. Promise me you'll take Rowdy and ride for your life. It means a lot to me. Promise!"

"I promise! But, Wes, you said yourself that Indians don't fight at night. Anyway, they may not know we're here."

"They know now. You can be sure they were watching the troops. Whether they attack or not depends on how they perceive our strength or weakness. Our most vulnerable time will be at dawn. If things go well tonight, we may be near enough to the fort by morning to make it in safely."

"Well, it looks like it's time. Here comes your father. Keep one of those revolvers close to your side, Lee, and keep a sharp eye."

He left her then, stopping to check his rifle and the ammunition in his sidearm. He stepped into the saddle and rode Rowdy to where Lieutenant Berry sat waiting.

8

THE SCOUT, a weather-beaten, rugged individual dressed in tobacco-stained buckskin, had pointed the calvacade in a southwesterly direction, riding somewhat ahead. Lee had taken note of him earlier as he stood off to one side, arms resting across the barrel of his buffalo gun, placed butt down on the ground. The handle of a knife protruded from his belt. Like all the others, his eyes, which were little more than slits in his face, kept scanning the horizons, only to return to her in wonder. Sitting on the seat beside her father, Lee had to smile at the comical way he rolled the chaw around in his mouth before spitting into the dust of the ground.

Slowly they made their way through the moonless night. She could hear the movement of the horses ahead, an occasional creaking of leather as someone shifted their weight, and the wheels of the wagon turning in desert sand. The men rode in silence, rifles resting across their saddles. No doubt, most had a finger on the trigger. The wail of a coyote so close to them startled her.

Wes checked Rowdy's gait and dropped back out of sight. Lee felt his weight as he climbed over the tailgate and up to the front. "I'll relieve you for a spell, sir," he said quietly in her father's ear.

Hiram Webster was only too glad to relinquish the reins. The tugging and pulling had made his wounded shoulder ache, and the strain was beginning to wear him down. He sat between them for a while. But tiring of this, he soon retired to his pallet in the rear.

"Lee, don't you be staying up too late," he whispered, in passing. "Tomorrow may be a hard day."

"All right, Pa," she responded, agreeably.

Once again, Lee found herself alone with Wes, who seemed to be giving his full attention to handling the team. Out of the corner of her eye she could see his profile etched against the dim sky. Curiously, her mind went back to the raven-haired, black-eyed girl who's picture was in the locket. Was she his sweetheart? If she was, why did he leave her to come to the West? Could it be she was out here somewhere?

She stole another glance at this man who sat beside her, conscious of how little she knew about him. He was from Georgia, the son of a sea captain, he had told her father. Yet, he did not talk like a Southerner. He had implied that because he had a sister, she could trust him. Yet, instinctively, she trusted Wes. What was it about him that made her feel comfortable in his presence? He was compassionate and thoughtful, yet, when confronted by an enemy, he could be quick and dangerous.

In comparison, she thought of the young men back home who had vied for her attention. They had wanted only to possess her, trying to take advantage of her every time they managed to get her alone. Uneducated farm boys and hunters for the most part, their needs were simple. They wanted a woman to tend their homes and bear their children. They could not understand her wanting more than that out of life. Mercy! What would they think if they could see her now, dressed in men's clothing, sitting beside a man with a big gun on his hip, and a revolver laying by her side. If they could only have seen her when she held the gun on those ruffians! She could almost see the horror-stricken face of Deacon Barden's daughter,

Olivia. The thought brought a smile to her face. Dear Olivia, what a bore she was.

Her reverie was interrupted by a cavalryman, riding back to notify them a brief halt had been ordered to rest the mounts and stretch their legs. Wes helped her down, and she welcomed the chance to walk a little. Her limbs felt stiff from sitting so long. "Stay close to the wagon," he warned, leaving her there.

In a short time, the musical jingle of spurs told her that Wes was returning. She could hear the men mounting, so she climbed into her seat. Wes stepped up and took his position beside her. He gave the horses a slap with the reins, and they were on the move again.

"Father is sleeping soundly. He didn't leave his bed," she murmured, looking back over her shoulder. "He's been doing a lot of that since mother died. The doctor told me it was his depression. I sure hope after all this he'll be better."

"Time has a way of taking care of things," Wes responded, quietly. Several moments went by before he spoke again.

"Lieutenant Berry says we'll start climbing soon, and it will be rough going. He wants to make it through the Peloncillo Pass before dawn. From there, it will level out until we reach the San Simeon River. Crossing shouldn't be a problem—it was dry when they came through there. You'll want to hold on pretty good. We don't want you falling out on your head again."

The remembrance of his daring rescue embarrassed her, causing her face to burn. She was grateful for the cool night air that fanned her hot cheeks.

There was no way to judge time in this wide expanse of earth and sky. But to Lee, it seemed the hours had flown by. They had been climbing for some time. She could tell by the way the horses were leaning into the harness. Soon they were brought to a standstill again, but no one dismounted. One of the cavalrymen took a position by the wagon. Lee could feel his eyes upon her often.

"Why have we stopped?" she whispered to Wes.

"We're probably getting close to the pass, and the Lieutenant is waiting on a report from the scout before entering it. He feels that the greatest risk of attack will be there."

Lee gasped and clutched his arm. He kicked himself silently for offering that last bit of information. Although, for her sake, it was best that she knew the risk. He put his strong hand over hers.

"Lee, if you know a prayer, you might want to say it now. We could be in for a bad time. It'll be best if you get in the back and lay down. Take that extra pistol with you, use it if you have to. You should awaken your father when we start in. Every man needs to have his own chance. Give him the other gun from under the seat, if he'll use it." Wes stopped speaking, to listen. He could hear the movement of horses ahead of him. "Go now!" he whispered hoarsely. "Pray that God will be with us all."

Lee grabbed the revolver by her side and hastened to obey. She woke her father and repeated what Wes had told her, handing him the gun.

"Lee, I can't kill another human being!" he protested.

"Father, it's kill or be killed!" she argued quietly.

"Nevertheless, I cannot shoot this weapon at another person. Let them kill me—and I didn't raise you to be a killer of men, either," he said, dropping the gun out the side of the moving wagon.

"Father, these men are trying to help us!" Lee cried in a passionate whisper. "While you sit wallowing in self-pity, they're willing to die for us! Since you refuse to help them fight, the least you can do is pray for them—if—if that's the only weapon you choose to use. You better pray for me too—if I am captured by Indians—it will be worse than death!"

"Lee—I—," he entreated, reaching an unsteady hand out to her.

She pushed it aside and sank back on her seat. The jolting wagon jarred her sore body, rattling her teeth. Through a rip in the tent covering, a star twinkled down at her. Many times she had heard her mother say, "The sun shines on the just and the unjust." Out there in the darkness, a band of Indians may be lurking to take their lives, while brave men rode through the night to protect them, and the same star shines on both.

Surely God would watch over them all! Hot tears flooded her eyes, running down upon her pillow. The events following her mother's death and the care of her father had consumed all her energies, mentally and physically. In those last lonely, confusing days, none had come to comfort her. Disillusioned with the church and its people, she had given little considera- tion to spiritual things. Silently, she fought the fear that as- sailed her by remembering snatches of scripture she had mem- orized as a child. Blessed relief came in repeating them over and over in her mind.

From where she lay, Lee could see Wes, leaning forward to tap the team of horses on their rumps with the ends of the reins, urging them forward. The quiet strength of him was a comfort to her. She felt her father's eyes staring at her in the dim light. However, he made no further attempt at conversa- tion. She knew her words had struck him deep, hurting him, but she was too distraught to feel her usual compassion for him. She was grateful when he decided to join Wes in the front, leaving her to be alone.

Wes offered no comment at Hiram Webster's presence. His mind was busy summing up their chance for survival. From the position of the North Star, he figured there was only about an hour of darkness left. The wagon was slowing their progress in the rough terrain. The sensible thing to do was to abandon it, take the horses, and ride out. He signaled the trooper nearest him.

"Take a message to Lieutenant Berry. Tell him we are go- ing to leave the wagon and ride the horses out. We'll have a better chance of making it that way." The man touched his hat and hastened forward.

"Mr. Webster, you and Lee gather any valuables you may have and tie them up in something that can hang on the pommel of your saddle. We are going to have to leave the rest of your belongings behind if we hope to make it out of here alive. Hurry!"

Wes pulled the team to a halt, noting the riders ahead had stopped. Jumping down, he ran to unhitch the horses, bringing them around to the rear of the wagon. In a matter of minutes he had them saddled and ready.

"Come, we must go," he called quietly to Lee and her father. Each appeared with a bundle they handed to Wes. He tied them to the saddle of the spare horse. Lee hopped to the ground and stood waiting for instructions, not daring to look at her father, who lingered, taking one last look around.

"Lee, here. Let me help you up on Rowdy," Wes said, leading the big chestnut over to where she was standing. When she was mounted, he hurriedly adjusted the stirrups and placed the reins into her hands, giving them a squeeze. "Stay close to me and remember your promise," he finished huskily, turning to help her father. "Take the mare, Mr. Webster, she's more rested."

Wes climbed aboard one of the team animals and picked up the reins of the other. At his signal that all was ready, they moved out at a rapid pace. Rowdy soon caught up with his master, content to stay abreast. Lee was glad she had always shared a love for horses with her mother, whose family raised fine stock. It was her grandfather who had taught her to ride like the wind. Rowdy's gait was smooth. Lee could feel the strength of the powerful horse beneath her. Despite the conditions under which she was traveling, she found herself thrilling to the ride on this wonderful animal. He beat any horse of her grandfather's she had ridden.

Before long, the pass narrowed somewhat. Over his shoulder, Wes could see the first graying of dawn. Lieutenant Berry must have seen it, also, for he increased their speed. The troops were riding by twos, leaning low in the saddle.

Lee turned to look back at her father. From what she could tell, he seemed to be faring well. A pang of remorse hit her as she remembered her angry words. She would have to make amends for that as soon as possible. When she returned her gaze to the front, it was to find the others ahead had come to an abrupt stop. She was grateful that Rowdy had already checked his pace.

Everyone sat as carved from stone, suspended in time. No one spoke. The heaving of the horses was the only sound to be heard. Suddenly, from the darkness ahead came the call of a bird—to be answered by another higher up. Lee cast a questioning glance at Wes. He had raised his rifle, poised as if ready to fire.

There was little time to reflect on his action, for a blood-curdling yell broke the silence, causing Rowdy to jump nervously. "Ride for it!" came the order. Horses jumped into action as riders applied the spurs. Rowdy leaped forward, almost upsetting her as he pushed his way through the riders racing before him. The whine of bullets speeding toward an unseen target filled the air. Lee felt something catch at her jacket sleeve, with the feeling of a bee sting, as the big chestnut thundered on through the opening of the pass and out into the desert beyond.

Looking back, she caught sight of two riders coming out at an angle to intercept her. Indians! They were going to try to catch her! Behind them, she could see a trail of dust indicating that others were coming from the pass. Could it be more Indians? Lee felt the blood constrict in her veins, and she reeled in the saddle. It was then she realized that in the first burst of speed, the scarf had blown from her head to leave her hair streaming in the wind. Despair and weakness threatened to overtake her. Only God and this wonderful horse could save her now!

Remembering Wes's instructions, she leaned low over Rowdy's shoulder. "Go, Rowdy, go," she screamed to him. She felt him respond effortlessly. The ground beneath them became a blur, and the wind tore at her clothes as he soon outdistanced her pursuers. When she saw the Indians give up the pursuit and turn back, Lee hauled back on the reins, bringing the stallion to a standstill. She watched as they were confronted with rifle fire from the horsemen who had followed them. Almost by magic, they faded into the desert.

Lee sat poised, ready to flee, when a call came from the riders striving to catch up with her. Rowdy reared his head as she heard a piercing whistle. Though she was unable to make out who it was, Lee knew by Rowdy's reaction that it had to be Wes. She could only hope the smaller figure beside him was her father. Rowdy pranced impatiently, but Lee held him in check, waiting.

$\mathcal{T}$HE SUN WAS JUST BREAKING THE HORIZON, highlighting the brooding Peloncillo Mountains with a golden glow, not yet penetrating the shadows in the desert floor, when Wes and Lee's father caught up with her. Rowdy whinnied a welcome at their approach. Wes spoke words of greeting to the horse, but his eyes were on Lee. Her pale face was showing the strain of a sleepless night and there was blood on her sleeve, but she was sitting straight, strangely composed, eyes bright. She sure was a game one, he thought, admiringly.

"Lee! Are you all right?" her father cried, dismounting to run over.

"You've been hurt!" Wes observed, endeavoring to restrain his feelings, but with concern showing in his voice.

"I don't think so," she replied, with a wan smile. "My arm hurts some. I—I think a cactus punctured my sleeve."

"Better let me take a look at it," Wes advised, climbing down. "Those thorns can be painful."

Hiram Webster tenderly helped his daughter down, steadying her on her feet. He assisted her out of her jacket and rolled up the shirt sleeve. There was a ragged-looking flesh wound in the upper part of her arm near the shoulder.

"That wound was made by a bullet!" Wes acknowledged grimly, not wanting to think about what a few more inches would have done. He untied the kerchief from around his neck and wet it with water from his canteen. With trembling hands, he cleansed the dried blood from the smooth white arm, avoiding her eyes, which studied his face. He took the salve from his saddlebag and applied some of it to the injury. Then, he tore off the sleeve of the shirt, making a bandage of it. All the while he felt Lee's disturbing eyes upon his face.

Not trusting himself any longer, he left her in Hiram Webster's care and strode off to watch the line of weary troops that were coming toward them. The old scout was far in the lead. A bloody bandage encircled his head. He pulled his drooping horse to a stop in front of Wes and pulled one leg up to lay over the saddle.

"Well, sonny, I allus feared them redskins would get my scalp eventually, and this time they jist about did. Iffen it warn't fer you, I'd be a gonner. Much obliged." He paused, directing his keen gaze at Lee. "How's the lass?"

"A bullet grazed her shoulder. I bound it up with some salve, but it'll be sore. Like all the rest of us, she needs rest."

"Aw, now," the older man breathed in genuine sympathy.

"How much farther is it to the fort?"

The scout squinted at the sun, then spat on the ground before answering. "I reckon 'bout half day's ride, moving kinda steady." He turned to look at the cavalry, which had almost caught up with them. "It's gonna be hard on them that's hurting, though. Iffen the lass is up to it, we'd best be moving on."

They had been riding for several hours, and the coolness of the morning had fled before the increasing heat of the sun. Men sagged in their saddles as the weary horses plodded along. Wes felt his eyes burning in their sockets. Hiram Webster seemed to be holding up pretty well, but Lee was swaying in such a way that it worried him. He called Rowdy to a halt, then left his horse, handing the halter to Webster. Freeing Lee's feet from the stirrups, he stepped up behind her and turned her sideways across the saddle, holding her tired body in his arms, setting off a riot of feeling in his chest.

"Come on, Rowdy, you can get us there," he muttered, in a voice choked with emotion.

The day was far spent when they arrived at the fort, a group of crude shelters made of adobe surrounded by walls of the same. They were greeted by the curious stares of an odd assortment of people. Soldiers in blue uniforms contrasted greatly with a number of Indians dressed in their colorful native garb. Scouts wearing their usual buckskin lounged on the porch of what Wes took for a trading post.

The golden-haired girl in the arms of the rider astride the big, chestnut-colored horse drew the most attention. Everyone stopped what they were doing to watch as they passed. Lieutenant Berry gave orders to fall out and take care of the wounded, then led the three of them to a low building in the middle of the parade grounds where a big, barrel-chested, gray-headed man in uniform was standing. He looked to be in his early 50s, with steely gray eyes that he shaded from the sun. Wes recognized him at once. Horace McDuggal!

"Captain, there was no sign of F company, but we found the scout," Lieutenant Berry reported. "His horse had drifted into the camp of these people. He was wounded pretty bad, had an arrow through the chest, but I think he'll pull through. We escorted these folks back and were attacked by hostiles in Peloncillo Pass. No loss of life, but some of the men suffered injuries. This is Hiram Webster and his daughter and—"

"Wes Scott! By the Lord Almighty! Is it really you? I thought you were dead—killed in that last skirmish on Cemetery Hill. When you've rested, I want to hear all about it," the captain greeted in a great, booming voice. He turned to address an aide standing nearby. "Corporal, lend a hand here. Take care of their horses."

Wes dismounted, still holding the girl in his arms. "She needs attention, Captain McDuggal," he said hoarsely, through dry, cracked lips.

"Of course! What am I thinking. Mary! Mary, come out here."

A handsome woman with graying hair appeared at the door to exclaim, "My lands, young man, bring the young lady in out of the sun, for goodness sake." Wes followed her into the cool interior of the post. "Here, lay her in here," she instructed, going into a small room furnished with a table, a chair, and a cot. She fluffed the pillow and pulled back the sheet.

Wes gently deposited Lee on the narrow bed, brushing the hair away from her face. Stepping back, he looked helplessly at Captain McDuggal and her father, who had followed them in.

"She's been hurt. Had a bad fall . . . then grazed by a bullet . . . I did what I could," Wes mumbled, brushing his hand across his eyes. He staggered toward the chair and fell to his knees, finally, stretching out prone on the floor.

"Corporal!" thundered the Captain, "Corporal! Get some help and take these men to quarters for some rest. See that they're not disturbed."

He remained to see the order carried out, following them through the door to watch as they carried Wes across the way.

"There goes a mighty good man," he said to an aide standing nearby, adding a warning. "See that he is treated well."

Captain McDuggal turned and reentered the building, his heavy tread shaking the floor as he walked to his office. He lowered himself into his chair and sat staring at the papers on his desk. Wes Scott! Let's see, he was under the command of Colonel Stothard. Yes, that was right. Always liked that boy! Wonder what he's doing out here? An angry voice in the outside office interrupted his thoughts.

"He'll see me, and he'll see me now!" the voice shouted angrily, followed by footsteps and the scraping of a chair.

A man of medium build, immaculately dressed in a black suit with a long coat strode into the office, followed by the protesting aide. His dark, handsome face, showing signs of dissipation, sported a neatly trimmed moustache. Narrowed, dark eyes darted suspiciously around the room, coming to rest on Captain McDuggal. He puffed long and hard on a cigar he held in his hand before speaking.

"Well, Captain, we meet at last. You are a hard man to see," he drawled sardonically.

"May I ask the meaning of this?" Captain McDuggal demanded.

"The meaning, Captain, is that I've been trying to see you and, according to your aides, you are too busy," the man replied with sarcasm evident in his voice.

"Who are you, and what is it you want?" queried McDuggal, making a mental note of the gun strapped against the man's right leg.

"Not much, really. I want you to provide safe passage for my wife and me to Fort Lowell at Tucson. I have business there," he answered, ignoring the first part of the question.

"I can't spare the men. C Company just had a bad scrape with Indians who tried to ambush them, and F Company hasn't come in off patrol yet. They're long overdue. Things are bad out there. It isn't safe to venture too far from the fort. I cannot grant your request," concluded Captain McDuggal, gruffly, standing to his feet.

Giving the captain an insolent look, the man rudely shook the ashes from his cigar on the floor before replying.

"Very well then, I'll hire some scouts to escort us," he exploded hotly, the blood rising in his face.

"There isn't a scout in this fort that would be that foolhardy," the officer countered with equal force, glaring at the man. "Corporal, show this man out!" he ordered abruptly.

"I'm leaving," the man ground out from between clenched teeth, freeing his arm from the grip of the aide who saw him out.

"Corporal Johnston, who is that man?" Captain McDuggal asked, looking up from his work to the returning aide.

"He is a gambler, sir. He goes by the name of Cromwell."

"He said he has a wife. Have you seen her?"

"Uh—yes, sir. She's—uh—young and pretty. Of course, all I know is what I hear rumored," the young man stammered, serious face growing a red hue.

"All right, Corporal."

The captain waved a hand in dismissal to the young man, who was only too glad to escape further questions on the subject, and sat looking out the window, eyebrows knitted together in deep thought. Cromwell. Where had he heard that name before? He searched his memory for facts but none materialized. Oh well, it would come to him later.

He got up and strolled out to the door of the post, squinting his eyes against the last slanting rays of the sun. It would soon be time for taps, signaling the end of another day. Where was the other company of troops? Had they met the same fate as their scout, or perhaps worse? The young lieutenant in charge was new to the ways of the desert and Indian warfare, but Sergeant O'Rourke was a seasoned fighter.

Loud voices coming from the porch of the trading post attracted his attention. Cromwell stood with his back toward him, gesturing with both hands as he talked with the group of scouts gathered there. From what Captain McDuggal could tell, Cromwell was meeting the negative response he predicted. What could be so urgent that he would need to leave the safety of the fort here?

His mind went to what Corporal Johnston had told him. He was not always privy to what his men did in their free time. Gambling was a pastime he knew about, but what else was the corporal alluding to? He decided Cromwell would bear watching. But who could he trust? The enlisted men stuck by one another. His breath caught in his throat. Why not Wes Scott? No one would suspect what he was up to.

Satisfied with his train of reasoning, Captain McDuggal returned to his quarters. Mary McDuggal greeted him with a fond smile as he entered the sitting room.

"How's the young lady?"

"I looked in on her just a few minutes ago—she's still asleep. The rest will be good for her. No doubt, she's been through a lot. I'll put a cot in there and stay with her tonight. She may be frightened when she awakes."

"Not a bad idea," he nodded agreeably, lowering himself into his favorite chair.

10

*W*ES OPENED HIS EYES to unfamiliar surroundings. The ceiling was of heavy beams and whitewashed adobe. The only light penetrating the dim interior came through a single window high on the opposite wall. He sat up and looked around the room. There was a table on which rested a candle and a book. Rumpled covers on a cot across from him gave evidence that someone had been sleeping there.

His worn boots had been removed and placed at the foot of the bed, along with his saddlebags. His hat and gun belt hung on a peg at the head. He could hear voices and the sound of people moving about outside. He pulled on his boots and walked to the window to peer out. As it all came back to him, he was shocked to find he had slept around the clock. He was at the fort. Lee—her father—they would be here too. Was it he who was sharing the room with him?

Wes opened the book to find it was a Bible belonging to Hiram Webster. It was not his nature to pry into things that were none of his business, but his curiosity caused him to turn the pages and read some of the notes written there. He had never seen a minister's Bible before. Often, he had wondered if it was the same as all the others. A crocheted strip in the Book of Isaiah marked the latest notation.

Wes held it up to the fading light. The words "a shadow from the heat" had been underlined. The notation read, "God hath overshadowed us from the heat and terror of the desert and hath delivered us." He put the book back in its place.

"Well, he's partly right, God, but You had a lot of help," Wes muttered, grinning as much as his sore lips would allow.

He rubbed his chin, surprised to find several days' stubble there. That was all right, he thought with satisfaction. It would make him less recognizable. He strapped on his gun belt, checking the shells in the chambers, then sat down to wait until the twilight had deepened before venturing out. If Testa and the gambler were here, he would not want them to know of his presence. Reaching for his saddlebags, he removed the locket, placing it in his shirt pocket.

He longed for some food but decided he would go see Captain McDuggal first to ask about Lee. Jamming his hat low over his face, Wes opened the door slowly. The small structure he was in stood on the same side as the post. Across the parade grounds, lights were coming from the trading post and another building, probably the mess hall. With a grunt of satisfaction he noted that most of the men were still at supper. Some were loitering on the porch of the trading post, others were sitting on the stoop outside their quarters.

Wes stepped out into the shadows, and as was the habit of a careful man, paused to listen to the sounds of activity around him. The plaintive, mournful notes of a harmonica struck a cord in his heart. How many times had he heard that sound on the battlefield, as forlorn young men played their music with thoughts of home and happier days.

Slipping around the corner, he walked up to the side of the post and sauntered out to mount the steps. There were lights in the outer office, but no one was there.

"Probably at mess," he murmured, going on through the room leading into the captain's quarters. The door was ajar when he knocked quietly. A woman's voice, followed by merry laughter, came from within. A heavy tread attested to Captain McDuggal's approach. The door swung wide.

"Well, well, so you did finally wake up! I've inquired about you several times today—was kinda worried. Come in, come in. There's a young lady here worrying about you too!"

"Can we talk in your office for a few minutes first?"

"Of course. Go on in—I'll excuse myself and join you there."

While he waited, Wes took the office in with a sweeping glance. A gun collection on the wall indicated the captain's interest in weapons. A Comanche bow and arrow hung alongside, telling a mute story. Behind the desk, which occupied the center of the room, hung a plaque and some medals. Two of them Wes recognized, for he had a couple just like them. A hall tree in the corner decorated with several items of uniforms and two chairs completed the furnishings.

When Captain McDuggal had seated himself at his desk, a broad smile creased his tanned face.

"It sure is good to see you, Wes. I didn't think I would ever see you again. When I saw you go down, just before I lost consciousness, I thought you were done for."

"Nor I you," he replied. "That day was a terrible time to be alive. The war should never have happened, but it did. I'm glad for the healing that has come to the country."

"What brings you out here?"

"Mac, have you ever seen this girl?" Wes asked, taking the locket from his pocket to hand to him.

Captain McDuggal flipped open the locket and studied the face in the picture. "She sure is a beauty. No, I can't say that I have. Who is she?"

"Her name is Testa—she's my sister. She broke our mother's heart when she ran off with a gambler. I promised mother I would find her and bring her back home if she was still alive. We—I have reason to believe all is not well with her from what I have been told along the trail. Testa was wild and headstrong, but she is not bad unless she is being forced—"

"She ran off with a gambler, huh?" Captain McDuggal asked with a frown, suddenly remembering his conversation with the corporal earlier.

"Corporal Johnston, come in here," he bellowed.

When no answer was forthcoming, he rose from his chair and went out. Wes could hear him talking to someone at the front. His face looked like a thundercloud when he returned, and he sat down drumming his fingers impatiently while waiting for the hapless corporal. Wes decided he would rather not be in Corporal Johnston's shoes at that moment.

Rapid footsteps sounded in the outer office, hesitating before coming on. When the corporal put in his appearance, his uniform was still in disarray. He seemed unusually flustered and ill at ease, his boyish face red with embarrassment.

"You—you sent for me, sir?" he managed to say with some difficulty.

"Yes, Corporal Johnston, why weren't you at your place of duty?" queried Captain McDuggal, glaring at him.

"I was delayed after mess, sir."

"Delayed, Corporal? When you finish here, remain in the outer office. We'll discuss this later," Captain McDuggal ordered coldly. "Now take a look at this picture. Have you seen this woman?"

Wes could not see the young man's face as he looked at Testa's picture, but he saw him stiffen perceptibly. He sensed the struggle going on in the corporal's mind as he weighed the consequences of denial. He had a hunch not only that Testa was here but that the man had fallen prey to her charm.

"Corporal Johnston," Wes interjected quietly, "the girl in that picture is my sister. She came from a fine Christian home and though strong-willed, she was good. A smooth-talking man, we later found to be a gambler, turned her head and she ran away with him. I have been trailing them, trying to save her before it's too late. I need your help. Have you seen her?"

The trooper had been in such an agitated state, he had taken little notice of Wes sitting there. Whirling to face Wes's steady gaze, his face blanched as the words sank into his troubled brain. He stumbled back to sink into the other chair, his legs no longer capable of holding him up. He buried his face in his hands.

"Yes," he said in a low voice, "I've seen her. She's here at the fort." He raised his head to look at Captain McDuggal before continuing. "She—I—uh—we were together tonight." He swallowed hard. "But it's not what you think. I really love her. I have asked her to marry me—but she laughed and said, 'You don't understand what I am—what he has made me!' I told her that I had heard rumors and I didn't care. I think she loves me, but there's something else—she's afraid of him."

"I understand, corporal," Wes said gently. "She is afraid for you. Be careful. Perhaps the two of us can save her. You've done well to take us into your confidence. I'm sure that Captain McDuggal will be lenient under the circumstances."

Glancing over at his friend, Wes was rewarded with a nod of agreement that wrought a great transformation in the miserable young man. Regaining his composure, he straightened in his chair. Hope replaced despair.

"What's your name, Corporal?"

"Tobias Johnston, sir. My friends call me Tobe."

"Well, Tobe, I don't want you to tell anyone about our talk tonight. If Blackwell finds out I'm here, they'll run, placing Testa in greater danger," Wes warned.

"He goes by the name of Cromwell here, and she calls herself Cresta," Tobe informed him.

"Yes, why not, he has been using other names all across the country," Wes mused out loud. "Where are they staying?"

"Over at the trading post. There's a couple of rooms on the back. She stays in the room nearest the door that opens to the outside. He spends evenings at the gambling tables while she—" Tobe's voice failed him. He brushed the dark hair from his forehead in a gesture of futility.

Wes knew what he was about to say. Cromwell used Testa to lure the men to the gambling tables using whatever means it took. He found his heart going out to Tobe, and he searched for words to lift his spirits. He did not doubt the sincerity in which the young man had made his declaration of love. Many before him had fallen hopelessly in love with Testa, but it was the redemptive quality of his love that struck a responsive chord in Wes.

Studying the serious boyish face, tanned by the desert sun, with its wide-set blue eyes, Wes liked what he saw. The cavalryman was of medium height, with a wiry body, tempered by the harsh environment of the Arizona frontier. His bearing led Wes to believe that the corporal had come from a good home. If Testa did love him—well—he would have to see.

The long silence was broken by Captain McDuggal, who dismissed the corporal. Wes sat staring at the floor, a plan of action taking form in his mind. He would try to see Testa tonight. But first, he wanted to see Lee. He picked up the locket from the desk and put it back into his pocket, then rose to his feet.

"How is Miss Webster, Mac?" he asked casually.

"She's getting along very well, Wes," he responded heartily, rising. "Her arm is still sore, but it's healing. The missus is glad to have her here for company. It's done wonders for the wife. Womenfolk get lonely out here. She's been asking about you. Come, I know she'd like to see you."

Wes followed him into the small living room where Mary McDuggal was sitting alone. She looked up from her handwork with a gracious smile of greeting.

"I'm begging your pardon for my appearance, ma'am," Wes found himself saying. He removed his hat, revealing an uncombed shock of sandy hair. "I have a reason."

"Mary, tell Angela there's someone to see her. Wes, if you'll excuse me, I'm going to turn in. Reveille comes early. Keep me informed—I want to know what's going on with this Cromwell. Good night!"

Left there with his hat in his hand, Wes felt a tinge of nostalgia as he looked around the room with its comfortable furnishings. Except for the Navajo rugs in the floor adding a touch of Western color, it reminded him of his mother. No doubt she was counting the days as they sped by, wondering. He would try to send a message to her if he had the opportunity to do so.

A light step behind him caused him to turn and stare in unbelief at the vision of loveliness he saw before him. Lee stood just inside the doorway. The white dress with its long, flowing skirt accented her slender figure. Her golden hair reflected the yellow light from the lamp giving the effect of a halo.

"Wes—! I've been so worried about you!" She came close to look up into his face. "Are—are you all right?"

He stood rooted to the spot, wretchedly aware of how he must look, not sure of himself. His hat fell from nerveless fingers. Her nearness caused his heart to swell as if it would burst. The blood pounded in his temples and ran like fire through his veins. Looking into her eyes, he felt like a drowning man. Her voice sounded far away.

"Wes—are you all right?" she repeated. Leaning closer, she touched his dry, cracked lips with her fingers. Their coolness felt like a balm. Her breath fanned his cheek.

"Girl—don't do that," he whispered hoarsely, taking her hands in his to keep from taking her into his arms.

She leaned her head against his breast. "Wes, you have been my protector, my savior, my shadow from the heat. Father told me how you carried me all that way." Her voice faded to a whisper. "When you didn't come to see me, I thought you had deserted me, that you were glad to rid yourself of caring for me. Then, Mrs. McDuggal told me what happened to you."

"Lee, you don't know what you're saying. God is the one who saved you—I was only an instrument."

"But you care for me, don't you?" she asked tremulously, leaning her head back to look in his eyes.

"Don't make it any harder for me than it is, Lee, I care a great deal for you. But I—"

"You don't love me—is that what you're trying to say, Wes?" She pulled her hands free and stepped back, pride coming to her rescue. Her face had lost its color, making her eyes appear dark and luminous. Never had she looked more beautiful.

"But you don't understand, there is something—someone I—I have given my word. There may be trouble. I could be killed," Wes stammered incoherently.

"It's the girl in the locket, isn't it? I'm sorry I've made such a fool of myself and embarrassed you. Wes, please forgive me."

"But that's not true—"

"Good-bye, Wes," she said with finality, and fled from the room.

Wes was dumbfounded. How did she know about Testa? He was at a loss to catch her meaning. Something he had said upset and hurt her. He knew in his heart that he cared a great deal for Lee, but he had never come to grips with his feelings for her. Always he had known there would be someone he could not walk away from. Lately, he had become more and more disenchanted with his lonely life. The long rides, the evenings by the camp fire, the solitude no longer held the contentment they once did. Was it because Lee had come to occupy a lot of his thoughts these recent days?

He picked up his hat and walked out, closing the door softly behind him. When he reached the outer office, he found that Corporal Johnston was still at his post, sitting with his chair tilted against the wall. Hearing the musical footsteps behind him, Tobe straightened up.

"It's all right, Tobe, relax. Say, would it be possible for you to rustle up something for me to eat?"

"Sure thing, Mr. Scott, be right back."

"Uh—Tobe, I'd rather no one knew my last name. Just refer to me as Wes."

The young man nodded in agreement and hurried out.

11

WHILE HE WAITED, Wes pondered over Lee's reaction to his visit. Surely she was distraught from all she had been through in the past few days. With her mother gone and a father caught up in his own world, she had turned to him. She needed to feel that someone cared. He could not and would not take advantage of her vulnerability, although he had to admit that her presence stirred him as no other woman had. Yet now, as it had been in the past, he could not afford to be distracted from the dangerous mission he was undertaking.

His mind went to Cromwell. There was no doubt that he was a dangerous man. He had left a bloody trail everywhere he had been. Although the deaths had been made to look like accidents or robberies, Wes felt that Cromwell had been behind them. Most had been at the table with him and won large sums of money. Others, particularly the younger ones, had unfortunately become infatuated with Testa.

Tobe returned with the food, and Wes wasted no time in getting on the outside of it. The coffee was strong and satisfying. Setting the plate aside, he rose to his feet.

"Much obliged, Tobe. Where's Rowdy being kept?"

"He's been turned in with Captain McDuggal's mount in the shelter near the corrals."

Wes pulled his hat low over his face and sauntered out into the night, going back the same way he came. But, instead of returning to his room, he went on in the direction of the stables. The small shelter housing Rowdy was straight ahead of him. Lifting the bar from across the door, he entered the dark interior. The smell of hay, horse liniment, and leather bore evidence of a clean stable. A low whistle drew a response from the big horse.

"Hello, boy," Wes said quietly, feeling his way to the stall. "How have they been treating you?"

He ran his hand over Rowdy's back and flank. Someone had curried him down. It was good to find each hoof had been trimmed, the shoes in good repair.

"Well, now, I'd say you've been faring pretty good," Wes muttered, letting Rowdy nuzzle his hand. "You just stay put and rest up. I'll take you out for a while in the morning."

He checked the location of his gear and silently let himself out, replacing the bar. Now to see Testa. Wes assumed a slouched appearance, shuffling a little as he walked toward the trading post. Loud laughter indicated that someone was bearing the brunt of an unseen joke.

Wes stepped into the dimly lit hall and scuffed over to lean on the counter. All eyes were on a young trooper, obviously under the influence of strong drink, who stood in a circle of men. He was trying to do a jig but could hardly lift a foot, much to the amusement of others. Another soldier was giving a pounding rendition of "Yankee Doodle" on an old, out-of-tune piano. Several were clapping their hands in time to the music.

Beyond them in a corner was a table surrounded by men, some sitting in the game, others looking on. In the middle with his back to the wall sat a tall man with narrowed, black, glittering eyes. Wes saw them move over him as they took in all that was going on in the room. His handsome face with its clipped moustache betrayed the evil that lurked in his heart. Appearing to be in a good mood, he was talking good-naturedly to those around the table to assuage any hard feelings they had over their losses. He certainly was a cool one.

Wes glanced around for Testa but didn't see her. The scraping of a chair turned his attention back to the game. One of the players had thrown his cards down and gotten to his feet quickly.

"I'm through, fellas I'm broke! I've lost my whole month's pay. No more for me. I'm going straight from now on." Resolutely he walked out.

It was then he saw Testa as she stood to her feet, tugging at the arm of a burly young cavalryman. She had been hidden from sight by the group in the middle of the place. Her appearance shocked him. Her once shapely figure was thin, and her eyes lacked their usual luster. Although she was still a beautiful woman, she had lost the youthful glow of innocence. He watched as she laughingly led the reluctant trooper to the empty chair. When he was seated, she stood behind him for a few minutes with her hands on his shoulders, watching as he was dealt a hand.

Wes kept his eyes on Cromwell, who gave the appearance of being unconcerned at her behavior. But when the trooper had his attention on his cards, Cromwell gave Testa a slight nod. She leaned over to whisper something in the man's ear, bringing chuckles from the rest of the men. Then, giving his arm a squeeze, she disappeared through the doorway leading to the back of the building.

When Wes looked back at Cromwell, he found the gambler was staring at him intently. He realized he had been caught watching Testa leave the room. Wes deliberately turned to engage a cavalryman nearby in a bit of conversation. When the trooper walked out, Wes went with him. He felt Cromwell's eyes on him as he left.

Once outside, he excused himself and walked off toward his quarters. Looking around, he was satisfied that no one was following him. Instead of entering his door, he paused to remove his spurs, leaving them by the door. The darkness at the side of the building hid his movement as he cautiously doubled back to the rear of the trading post.

He found the door ajar and was about to enter when he heard the low, angry voice of a man.

"Whadda' ya mean, go away. You were actin' like you wanted me to look you up later. Aw, come on, let me in."

"I said go away. If Cromwell finds you here, he'll make it hard on both of us. Please go! He'll be here any minute," came Testa's pleading reply.

Wes stepped quickly into the shadows as he heard steps coming out the door. A dark shadow moved away. When he was sure he would not be detected, Wes entered and tapped on Testa's door. He heard her groan, and then the door jerked open.

"I told you to go away!" she cried in a loud whisper.

"Testa, it's Wes," he said softly, pushing her back into the small room, closing the door.

"Wes?" she repeated after him, uncertainly.

He took off his hat so the light from the lamp would reveal his features. Testa came close so she could see him better, her face lit with recognition.

"Wes, it is you! Oh, Wes, why didn't you come—sooner!" Her voice broke into a sob, and she sank on the bed. "I looked for you every day at first, after I found out what he was—the devil himself. But he kept moving on every few days, farther and farther away, and I gave up hope. How did you find me way out here?"

"Mother sent for me, and I left immediately. I picked up your trail in New Orleans and have been on it ever since."

"Mother! Is she all right, Wes?"

"She was well when I left. But that's been a long time ago now."

"Oh, how can she ever forgive me?"

"She will, Testa, you know that."

"But—you don't know what I've been—what I've done."

Tears filled her eyes again and dropped off into her lap. Wes took her hands in his.

"I know all there is to know, Testa, but Mother need never know unless you want to tell her. Now we must make plans to get you away from this place. I have friends here. They'll help me. Don't tell anyone who I am. Keep a few of your things together, and be ready when the time comes.

"One more thing I want to know. Corporal Tobias Johnston says he is in love with you—he thinks you love him. Is this true?"

"Yes, he has asked me to marry me."

"Do you love him?"

"Too much to let him marry me. Besides, Cromwell would see that something bad happened to him. I told him tonight it wouldn't work—to forget me."

"I have one more question. Are you married to Blackwell, or Cromwell as he calls himself now?"

Testa dropped her head and answered in a low whisper, "No. He promised we would be married that first night, but then he said he had to make a rush business trip to New Orleans, and we would be married there. But we never were. He only acts like we are man and wife when it suits his purpose. I hate him!" she finished vehemently, trembling uncontrollably.

"Just hold steady, Testa, you'll be free soon," Wes said darkly.

"Ssssh! Oh no! He's coming. I can tell his footsteps. Wes, he can't find you here!"

Wes glanced around the room furnished only with a bed and an old ladderback chair. The bed was built too close to the floor for his big frame to fit under it. A small window opened to the back of the building. Wes eyed it dubiously. It was his only way out. The footsteps paused at the room next door, then continued on.

"Stall him, Testa. Tell him you're in bed," Wes whispered.

He blew out the lamp and raised the window. It would be a tight squeeze, but he could make it. He had one leg over the sill when Cromwell called to Testa, who had stretched out on the bed.

"Cresta. What are you doing?"

"Steady!" Wes warned gently.

"I just got in bed," she said in a tired voice.

Wes was just about all the way through when his belt buckle caught on the sill, making a noise. His heart froze. He realized he would be caught like a rat in a trap if Cromwell stepped out the back to catch him half out the window. He would not even be able to defend himself with his arms inside the room.

"Who's in there with you? Open this door, now!"

"Just a minute until I light the lamp. Oh, where are those matches."

"Never mind the lamp. Open the door now!" Cromwell ordered angrily, banging on the door.

Wes finally worked his shoulders out the narrow opening and dropped lightly to the ground below where he crouched, listening, gun drawn. The chair clattered to the floor.

"Oh, look what you've made me do. I think I've broken my toe! Oh!" Wes was satisfied Testa was acting. He could not hold back a grin even though he was worried about what the gambler might do. He heard her open the door for Cromwell, who charged into the room.

"What's been going on in here? Light the lamp!"

"Nothing until you got here," Testa retorted, lighting the lamp. "I have a headache, and it was so hot in here I opened the window for some air."

The creaking of the bed told Wes she had sat down on it.

"Now thanks to you, I've got a toe ache and a headache!" she complained.

"Well, you get some sleep, 'cause you're going to need it for tomorrow," Cromwell instructed.

When his footsteps left the room, Wes left his listening post beneath the window and backed away into the shadows. He could see the red glow of Cromwell's cigar as he stood in the back door. It arced to the ground in a shower of sparks as he threw it down and closed the door, turning the key in the lock. Wes stalked away knowing that for the present, Testa was safe.

. Most of the post was quiet except for the men on guard duty. Wes could see them silhouetted against the starlit sky. He paused beside the door to his adobe hut, picked up his spurs, and with soft tread slipped inside. Webster was in his bed and appeared to be asleep. Weary and excited, he sought his bed. Two beautiful faces floated before him in his last waking moment. One with eloquent eyes of love, the other, sad and tragic.

12

*L*YING IN THE DARKNESS OF HER ROOM, Lee listened with mixed emotions to the quiet jingling step that announced Wes's departure. Embarrassment assailed her time and time again, as she realized she had mistaken his kindness and concern for her welfare as love. How could he love her? His heart belonged to another.

But what about her own feelings? Was her attraction to Wes an infatuation? True, she had never been around a man of his caliber. The respect he had shown her had never been afforded her before by any man. Woman that she was, she knew that her appearance tonight had affected him greatly. Had she taken advantage of him under the circumstances? No, she denied hotly! She had been honest in expressing what she truly felt in her heart. I love him. God help me, I love him!

Burying her face in the pillow, Lee was tormented by the fact that she loved this man as she had no other, and he was walking out of her life forever. She could not imagine a day without being near him, sharing his life, caring for him. Tears came to her eyes and great sobs racked her body until late in the night. She lay empty and spent. Mercifully, sleep came to her rescue.

She awoke to a gray, sunless sky that matched her mood as she mechanically dressed, lingering longer than she needed so the others would have eaten and gone. A strong wind was blowing sand that beat against the window. Tumbleweeds were rolling erratically wherever the wind would take them.

Lee was having a late breakfast when she heard Mrs. McDuggal greet her father. He appeared excited when he joined her at the table to receive a cup of coffee offered by his hostess. Looking well and rested, he waited until Mary McDuggal left them alone before he spoke.

"Lee, I've got great news! A man and his wife, along with several others, will be leaving for Fort Lowell at Tucson tonight. They've agreed to let us go with them. We can take several of the horses and travel light. I've been told it isn't far."

"But—the Indians—there's danger!"

"These are hardy western men who know the desert, and they have assured me that they would not undertake the trip if there was any real danger out there. I told them we had money to pay our way. They seemed real glad to have us go along. It's our chance, Lee, to get away from this forsaken outpost."

"Father! How do you know you can trust these people? Why do we have to leave tonight?"

"They said it's easier to travel in the desert at night."

"I don't know, Father, maybe we ought to wait until we can go with an escort. Captain McDuggal assured me that he would see that we got there safely."

Rev. Webster looked at his daughter's pale face, noting the shadows there. It had been a long time since he had seen her happy. Now he felt their journey in the desert was about over. This very morning he had prayed that God would deliver them, and here was their opportunity to move on.

"Is there a reason you don't want to leave this place?" he asked gently.

Not wishing him to see the pain in her eyes, Lee picked up her plate and took it to the sink before answering. Her heart felt heavy in her breast.

"No, there's no reason for me to remain here any longer. I'll be ready."

"Good. I'll come for you later. Until then, you had better rest. You still look tired."

"How's the arm?" he asked, picking up his hat to leave.

"It's healing all right. It doesn't bother me any," she answered, turning to face him.

"Lee, you've stood by me when I was down. I want to make things easier for you from now on. You were right about me wallowing in my self-pity. You helped me see myself. I've been praying that God would help me be a better father. Remember what your mother used to say when we were going through trials? 'God will be a shadow from the heat. He will take us under his wings and protect us.' There are better times ahead, Lee. Be encouraged."

When she did not respond, he walked from the room and she could hear him thanking Mrs. McDuggal for the coffee. When he had gone, she washed and put away her dish, then returned to her room to pack what few belongings she had, leaving out the pants and old coat she had worn before. When that was done she sat staring out the window. There was little hope that she would see Wes again before leaving.

Lee spent the day at various tasks the captain's wife allowed her to do. Being busy helped the time pass and kept her mind occupied. However, she found it difficult to keep her eyes off the door when there were footsteps in the hall outside, causing her heart to pound.

Dinner that evening was a cheerful affair. Captain McDuggal was in high spirits, owing it to the fact that F Company had arrived back at the fort with few injuries sustained.

"They exchanged fire with a small band of hostiles, but failed to take any prisoners. They had been delayed helping a group of settlers to safety. All the men need a well-deserved rest," he explained happily.

He even teased Lee for sleeping so late. When he had retired to the sitting room, Lee helped clear the table and put away the food. A knock at the door told her that her father had come for her. Mrs. McDuggal dried her hands on the apron she wore and went to let him in.

"Good evening, Mrs. McDuggal. I've come to take Lee for a walk. I thought some fresh air would be good for her."

"Of course, Rev. Webster, I'll tell her you are here."

"Angela, your father is here to take you for a walk. I can finish what's left, you go along," she urged, taking the towel from Lee's hands.

Lee hurried to her room, passing her father who put a warning finger to his lips. As she quickly changed into the old coat and pants, she realized he did not want her to let the McDuggals know they were leaving for good. In her heart she felt that the whole thing was wrong—that they should wait and go with an escort. But, then—that would mean she would have to face Wes again. She couldn't stay inside forever.

When she returned to where he stood waiting, her father took her bundle and quickly drew her out, closing the door softly. Taking her by the arm, he led her through the back door and walked swiftly to the rear of the trading post where horses were saddled and waiting. Lee recognized the horses they had ridden in.

Hiram Webster tied her things on the pommel of the one he had chosen for her to ride, then mounted up, indicating she should do the same. They were soon joined by the others who followed suit and silently they headed out. Most of the men were in the mess hall, and they seemed to draw little attention as they passed through the gate, causing Lee to wonder. From what she could tell in the dark, there seemed to be five men including her father, and a smaller form, which she took to be the wife of one of them.

After walking their horses for some distance, they broke into a fast trot, riding close together. It did not go unnoticed by Lee that she and her father were surrounded by a rider on each side and one in the rear. Something in their demeanor made her uneasy. Crediting it to her emotional state, she tried

to put it from her mind. Surely they were just looking out for
their welfare. After all, there was another woman in the party.

On and on they rode through the night until Lee felt
every bone in her body was being jolted. A cool wind was
blowing, forcing her to button her coat high around her neck,
making her hands so cold and stiff she could scarcely hold the
reins. The clouds which had lingered all day were breaking up,
and here and there she could see stars shining through,
promising a sunny day tomorrow.

When dawn broke clear and cold, they were still pushing
onward at a relentless pace. With the coming of daylight she
could see a close range of mountains rising up out of the
desert floor. A patch of green at the base indicated water was
there. Surely they would stop to rest and stretch their legs for a
while, Lee reasoned to herself. She was so tired and sore that
she reeled in the saddle and would have fallen had her father
not called her name.

Fighting to stay awake, she studied the rest of the riders
in the group. Up to now, those she had ridden with all night
had been dim outlines in the darkness. No one had spoken
during the entire trip except her father. The slender form of
the woman ahead swayed suspiciously back and forth with the
movement of her mount. She rode with her head down, shoulders drooping. Black braids of hair hung down her back.
Dressed in a khaki riding suit, she resembled an Indian. The
big man who rode by her side paid little heed to her discom-
fort.

Lee shifted her gaze to the man astride the horse on her
right. He was of medium build, with a distinct hawkish profile
that bore a short stubble of beard. His hat was pulled low over
his face, so she could not see his eyes. If he knew she was
looking at him, he gave no indication. He wore two big black-
handled guns on each side, tied down, as was the custom of a
gunman. They looked so sinister that Lee felt her flesh crawl.

She could not tell much about the rider on the left, except
he was smaller in stature. He, too, gave the appearance that he

was unaware of her presence. She resisted the urge to turn and look at the one who rode in the rear. She found it strange that they had not changed positions all night.

Lee thought of the revolver she had wrapped in a piece of clothing in her bundle. She would have to guard against its discovery. A feeling of regret struck a deep chord within her as she remembered it was Wes who had insisted she keep the weapon near her for protection. She wondered where he was.

With great effort, she pushed the disturbing thoughts from her mind, giving her attention to the mountains that loomed over them. The peaks were lit up in bold relief by the first golden rays of the morning sun. The green she had seen earlier turned out to be a grove of cottonwood trees, which proved to be a welcome sight. Lee observed a covey of quail slipping away among the creosote bushes, protesting noisily. She never tired of watching them. The males, who looked like tiny Roman soldiers in plumed helmets, constantly bobbed their heads in communication with their mate.

A cry brought her out of her reverie. The man to the left was pointing to the south where a trail of dust was rising in the still morning air. There were horses coming toward them at a fast rate of speed.

"Ride!" shouted the man in the back.

No other urging was needed as they prodded their tired mounts into a mad dash toward the safety of the trees. As they thundered in under the trees, the men were already leaping from their saddles, guns in hand. The big man who had been in the lead seemed to be in command.

"Webster! Take those horses out of sight! You men find cover and hold your fire! You women get off those horses and go up in the rocks! Stay down until we call you!"

His bold black eyes swept over Lee as she sat paralyzed with fear. What she saw expressed in them was repugnant. He started toward her, but the rider who had ridden by her side all night came to her aid.

"I'll help her down, Cromwell, you'd best be helping your woman. Here yuh go, Miss, it'll be hard standing on your feet at first after such a long ride, but yuh have t' hurry along."

Lee stumbled along to follow the man called Cromwell and the woman he was half carrying into the shelter of some rocks. Her father was gathering the horses, making ready to lead them away.

"Pa, give me my bundle!"

"Why would you want that at a time like this?"

"Don't ask, Father, just give it to me!" she insisted, taking it from him as he reluctantly handed it to her.

"Come!" the man called Cromwell shouted to her.

Lee hurried to obey, already aware of drumming hoofbeats drawing nearer. Cromwell pushed her down behind a rock and ran to take up a position behind a fallen tree. Watching his retreating figure, Lee intuitively felt him a dangerous man to be reckoned with.

When the sound of approaching horses suddenly ceased, a deadly silence settled on those who waited in their coverts. Lee could hear the quiet sobbing of the woman near her. With all her fear and misgivings, it did not occur to her to resort to tears. Instead, she knew that she must keep her wits to face what lay ahead, for with certainty she sensed a terrible foreboding of what was about to happen.

With trembling fingers, Lee untied the bundle she had brought, removed the gun placed there the night she had left the wagon, then retied the knot. She had never fired a pistol before, and she sat looking at it, trying to remember what Wes had done. His reaction had always been so swift she had never really seen him pull the hammer back.

She was dismayed to find there were only three bullets left when she checked the cylinder, but that was better than nothing. She stuck the gun in her waistband and buttoned her coat over it. If all else failed, she decided grimly, she would save the last shot for herself.

Raising herself on her hands and knees, she ventured a peek to see what was going on. Her father was nowhere to be seen. He must have stayed with the horses. A shot rang out, accompanied by a terrifying cry. More shots followed and she saw Cromwell raise his arm to fire at an unseen enemy. A groan told her that another bullet had found its mark.

Horrified, she saw one after another of the men fall, their guns firing wildly. One of the bullets struck the rock, just inches from her face, showering her with fragments. She heard a gasping cry from the woman opposite her. Poor dear, she was probably scared to death.

Cromwell appeared to be the only one remaining to defend them. He kept firing methodically in first one direction, then another. His revolver clicked on empty. Lee heard him swear an oath as he attempted to reload. The firing suddenly stopped, leaving a pall of smoke drifting among the trees. Cromwell stood transfixed, listening. Soon the sound of horses moving away brought a long expulsion of breath from him, and he stepped out into the open.

Lee watched as he strode forward, gun hand down at his side, face gleaming in the sun. He had taken only a few steps when he was cut down in a hail of lead. Dark-skinned bodies, which had been invisible only seconds before, emerged to take coup, dancing in fiendish glee, holding their trophy high. Sickened by the sight, she yielded to the blackness that enveloped her.

When consciousness returned, Lee's first sensation was of pain. Her face was hurting, there was a taste of blood in her mouth and the smell of dirt was in her nostrils. She must have fallen facedown. The horror of what had happened returned as she tried to remember how she had gotten there.

"Please, dear God, please don't let them find us!" she silently prayed.

How long she remained there listening for the slightest sound, Lee did not know. She was afraid to move for fear of discovery. A groan came from someone close by. It was then she remembered the woman who had hidden behind the rock close to her. She lifted her head and raised herself slowly to her knees again, peering over the rock. There was no one in sight. Cromwell lay where he had fallen, a ghastly sight, causing Lee to shudder. Dare she leave her hiding place?

She ducked back down to think. The sun was nearly overhead now. They had ridden in here just after sunup. That would mean that nearly five hours had elapsed. Father! He had taken the horses away. Had he escaped? A cold dread squeezed her heart.

The woman groaned again. Lee realized she would have to go to her aid before she cried out. Either way, it was a risk she decided to take. She took another look around, patiently studying every bush and tree as Wes had taught her. A bird flew down from a tree to perch on a shrub before hopping to the ground. That was a good sign.

Quaking inwardly with fear, she scurried to the woman's side. She was curled up in a fetal position with her face between her arms. The side of her riding habit showed that she had been bleeding. The bullet that had hit the rock above her head must have ricocheted, hitting the woman.

Lee turned her over on her back. Gasping in amazement, she sat back on her heels, staring at the face before her. It was the same likeness that had smiled at her from the picture in the locket, only thinner! It was she Wes had come west to find. How great a love he must have for her!

Carefully she loosened the blood-soaked clothing. The bullet had entered the lower left of the back coming out under the ribs in the abdomen. She had lost a lot of blood. Water! She would need water to cleanse the wound. Trembling with fear, Lee stood slowly to her feet. Her legs were shaking so badly, they did not want to bear her weight. Hesitantly she started forward, averting her eyes so as not to see Cromwell. Creeping among the trees and bushes, she searched for water. Only when she had found the shallow pool did it occur to her that she had nothing to carry water in. Perhaps she could use one of the canteens.

Her heart pounded as she went in the direction she had seen her father take the horses. She did not see him at first, for he was laying in a wide crack in the rocks. With a cry she ran to kneel by his side. His arms were outstretched. In one hand he held a canteen, the other, the gold cross he usually wore around his neck. Had he thought that would stop them? Lee felt numb as she sat beside him. At last, he had found the peace he had sought so long. Now he was with her mother. She slipped the canteen and the gold cross from his fingers and made her way back to the rocks.

The sun was growing hot, and she knew she would have to get the woman in the shade. It would be too dangerous to move her. Somehow she would have to build a shelter to protect her from the heat. Among the trees, she found some fallen limbs. Working as fast as she could, she placed them in the ground and stacked rocks to hold them upright. From her bundle she took the white dress and petticoat she had worn the night before. Ripping it down the middle, she tied each corner to a stick. The shade was scanty, but it was enough.

This done, she bathed the wounds and bound them up with strips she had torn from her petticoat. Now there was nothing to do but watch and wait. Taking up her lonely vigil, Lee refused to accept the fact that they might both die here in this lonely place. Had she not heard her father say, "God's eyes are upon his children and his ear is open to their cry"?

The woman stirred restlessly. Lee bathed her lips with water from the canteen.

"Wes—you did come," she murmured weakly.

13

*W*ES AWAKENED AT FIRST LIGHT. From somewhere on the post came the crowing of a rooster. It surprised him. It was a sound he had not heard for a long time. Quietly, he sat up on the side of his cot. Webster was sound asleep, breathing heavily.

Today he would lay plans to steal Testa away and hide her. He would need the help of Tobe and Captain McDuggal to pull it off. It was urgent that he see them as soon as possible. Dressing quietly, he put on his hat, picked up his boots and gun belt, and slipped barefoot from the room. He was met by a stiff, cool breeze blowing in from the northwest. The morning sky was covered with clouds. He leaned against the building to pull on his boots, then headed out, strapping on his belt as he walked.

A light was on in the mess hall, and he headed that way. It was almost time for reveille. Most were still sleeping soundly in their bunks. Except for the guards who were no doubt looking forward to their relief from duty, few were stirring. The cook, a wizened, genial fellow, hailed him with a friendly greeting.

"Well, cowboy! I see you're up mighty early. Must've smelled my coffee, huh? Hep yerself! How 'bout some solids t' go with it?"

Wes poured himself a cup, nodding his acceptance of the offer. Leaning against the counter, he passed the time in pleasant conversation while watching the man put together a plate of food for him.

When he had satisfied his hunger, Wes thanked the cook and sauntered casually from the building just as the trumpeter sounded the wake-up call. It brought back memories of many mornings he had hated to leave his bed after a long day of fighting. Many of these men, raw recruits, were learning life the hard way here in this harsh desert environment. Whatever fantasies they may have had of the grandeur of life on the Western frontier would quickly be dispelled.

He swung by the stables to look in on Rowdy and give him a piece of sugar he had saved from breakfast. The big horse whinnied his greeting. Wes ran his hands over the smooth chestnut coat as Rowdy nuzzled the treat from his hand.

"Rowdy, I do declare, you're going to get so used to this easy life, you might just run away and join the army!" he exclaimed softly.

Checking his tack, he found the saddle had been cleaned and polished. His canteen, filled with water, hung on a nail nearby. He whistled under his breath.

"Boy, Rowdy, you're not the only one living high on the hog, fella. When I was in the army, I had to do all this myself. Just enjoy it. Time is coming when we'll be back on the trail, just you and me."

Giving the horse a final pat on the rump, Wes left by the rear door opening out in the corral where he slipped through the bars and proceeded up to the office. So far as he could tell, his action was seen only by the guards on duty in the stockade.

No one was there for the moment, but he could see Tobe returning from mess. Wes waited patiently while he stopped briefly to talk to another soldier, before coming on. He liked the looks of this young man. If Testa would have him, he would make a fine addition to the family. Tobe's eyes lit up when he saw Wes standing there.

"Morning, Mr. Scott."

"Tobe," Wes replied with a nod of greeting. "I wanted to have a talk with you and Captain McDuggal to let you in on the plans to save Testa. Can that be arranged sometime this morning?"

"I'll see if the captain is in his office, sir."

"Thanks. Call me Wes."

"Yes, sir!"

Wes chuckled as he rubbed the stubble on his chin. There was an old mirror on the wall behind Tobe's desk. While he waited for Tobe to return, he walked over to take a look at himself. The beard made him look much older. Well, at least he looked the part. He would be glad to get this over and get a shave. Judging by his shabby appearance, he could use a bath and some new clothes. Tobe returned to tell him Captain McDuggal was anxious to see him.

"Tobe, you come in too. I'll need your help in getting Testa out of Cromwell's grasp."

When the three of them were seated in McDuggal's office, Wes laid out his plan. If possible, he wanted to avoid a confrontation. There was no need for anyone to be hurt, least of all Testa. Tobe was to see that Testa got a note from Wes informing her that she should pack her things and wait for him in her room. He would come for her after Cromwell had gone to bed.

The hardest part, he explained, was to find a place to hide her until Cromwell moved on or they could ride out with an escort.

"There is a simple solution to that," Captain McDuggal spoke up. "She can stay with us. No one need know. Mary would love to have two womenfolk around."

"That's mighty decent of you, Captain. She will need a woman's care. Lee will be good for her too. Just keep her out of sight."

"You can count on us to do our part, Wes."

"Good. Now, Tobe, if you'll get me some writing material, I'll write that note," Wes said, getting to his feet to follow the corporal into his office.

Tobe brought him the supplies, and he sat down in a chair to labor over what he wanted to say. When he had finished, he folded the paper and handed it to Corporal Johnston.

"Be real careful with that, Tobe. All could be lost if it falls into Cromwell's hands."

He stood to his feet and glanced out the window. Across the parade ground, Cromwell was standing on the porch of the trading post, smoking a cigar. Common to his gambler breed, nothing would escape his attention. So, to avoid his scrutiny, Wes thought it best to exit through the back entrance. He was just about to turn away when he saw Hiram Webster walk up to Cromwell. The two appeared to know one another, gesturing as they talked. Somehow it didn't strike Wes right as he turned away, but it was none of his business.

"I'll be back right after dark, Tobe. Can you have some food here for me?"

"Sure, sir—uh, Wes."

Wes went down the hall, waving a hand at Captain McDuggal, who looked up from his paperwork as he went by. He was about to let himself out when he thought about the injured scout he had saved. Retracing his steps, he stopped at the door of the office.

"Mac, where would I find that Indian scout we brought in? I thought I'd look in on him."

"He's in the infirmary right next door, if he's still there. They tell me they've had a hard time keeping him down. You can go right out this door and into the back of the building."

When Wes inquired, Joe was gone. The orderly explained good-naturedly that Indians did not like to be indoors much. They felt that sleeping out in the open air was more healing. Speaking of healing, he went on to tell Wes that some of the Indian's friends brought in some leaves and put on his wounds. It seems they had more faith in their medicine than ours. Whatever it was, Joe seemed to get better fast.

Wes lingered for more than an hour, talking with the man who was a fountain of information. He had been one of the many Negro soldiers that had made up the 54th regiment from Massachusetts, the first all-black unit, who had volunteered to fight for the union. He had become a pony soldier because he had no one to go back to. His family had all died in slavery. The army had become his family. It was a story Wes had heard before.

"What's your name, soldier?"

"Abraham. Like the one who set my people free."

"Well, Abraham, you're a good man, and I've enjoyed talking to you. Guess I'll be moving on now. You take care."

Wes moved off in the direction of his quarters. As far as he could tell, Cromwell was nowhere in sight. But still he must be careful not to spook him so that he would run. That would be very dangerous for Testa. He could only hope his presence was not known. He would rest and wait until dark before venturing forth. Reaching the door, he found it had been left ajar. He pulled his gun and stepped to one side.

"No danger," spoke a deep, guttural voice from within.

Wes sheathed his gun and stepped into the room. Joe, the scout, stood at the end of his bed, arms folded, face in calm repose. Black eyes somberly regarded him.

"I wait for you."

"I just went by the infirmary to see you. Abraham told me you had left. I'm glad to see you're better, Joe."

"Joe is my army name—my real name is Red Hawk. You saved my life. It is yours."

"No man's life belongs to another, Red Hawk. I will be your friend—your brother, nothing more," Wes replied fervently, in a ringing voice.

"You—me—brothers!" Red Hawk spoke emphatically, gesturing with his hands.

"Well now, that's fine with me," Wes responded with a boyish grin. "What tribe is your people?"

"My people no longer roam free. They are scattered far from their homeland, and their ways are no more. They are adopting the ways of the white man. I am Cherokee."

There was a note of sadness in his voice. Wes was at a loss to reply.

"I go now. I stay near."

After the Indian had stalked noiselessly out, Wes sat in deep contemplation. The Cherokee nation was one of the few civilized tribes who met the expanding white culture by adopting Christianity and the white man's ways. Their homelands were supposed to be protected by a treaty with the government, but the white man had put such pressure on the president that they had been driven from their lands in western Georgia to a new territory in the windswept plains of Oklahoma.

He remembered the stories he had heard of their treatment by the soldiers. Dragged from their homes, they were driven at bayonet point like cattle to wagons and taken westward. Many had died from the cold and starvation.

Red Hawk was an enigma. Here he was, serving as a scout for the very army that had displaced his people. Why would he do that?

He shook his head, admitting gravely that man's inhumanity to man had brought about much suffering to the human race. Fondly, he remembered his father championing the cause for many a luckless sailor. Though he had his father's Corsican blood flowing in his veins, it was from his gentle mother that Wes took his temperament. Aside from the terrible war between the states, he had always tried to help those who were in trouble.

His mind went to Lee and her father. Where would they go from here? The thought of them going on without him caused a tumult in his breast. It would mean he would never see them again. A feeling akin to panic triggered something deep inside of him, and he trembled. Lee's face with its imploring eyes floated before him. He recalled the touch of her cool fingers on his sore, sunburned lips, the fragrance of her hair as she leaned against him, her confession of love.

Wes got to his feet and walked unsteadily to the window. What could he have been thinking? Confused and shaken, he had not understood that she was baring her soul to him. Was it because of his stubborn resolve to save Testa that he had failed to see how he had hurt her?

"It's the girl in the locket, isn't it?" she had asked.

Only now did the full meaning of her question dawn on him. His behavior had led her to believe he was in love with the girl in the locket! That was why her face had lost its color and she had fled from the room.

Racked with a tormenting storm of emotions, Wes backed away to drop helplessly on his cot, his face in his hands. As he dealt honestly with each accusing thought, he came to the realization that he was hopelessly in love with Lee. What was it the McDuggals had called her? Angela! He liked that name better—it suited her better. She had an inner strength and fire that would make a man proud to stand by her side. Outside of his mother, she was the only woman he had ever loved, and man that he was, he had misunderstood what she was trying to tell him last night. He would make it up to her when he took Testa over tonight.

When he finally raised his head, the hour was growing late. Tobe would be bringing supper back for him soon. In the dim light remaining, Wes checked his gun and stood watching from his window. He leaned his hand on the table and discovered Webster's Bible was no longer laying there. In fact none of his things were laying about as they had been. Well aware that Webster did not especially like him, Wes assumed he had sought another place to stay. Seeing him together with Cromwell this morning had been troubling. He could only hope the man would not do something foolish to endanger himself and Lee.

When darkness had fallen at last, Wes let himself out in the cool night air and began his roundabout trek to the post, going by the stable where he paused long enough to saddle Rowdy.

"We just may have to make a run for it, boy, so you be ready," he muttered, hanging his canteen on the pommel.

He departed through the rear door of the stable and found his way out through the corrals, gently nudging the horses aside. Music from the battered piano in the trading post announced that the evening of revelry had begun. Someone lustily sang out their rendition of a song about home and loved ones far away. Wes grunted as he recognized the song. It made him think of his own home so far away. Soon this trail would end and he would go back. His heart quickened at the thought.

He tried the rear entrance to the office, but the door was bolted. Patiently, he made his way to the front, feeling his way in the dark between the buildings. He paused in the shadows just outside the door to listen before stepping into the lighted room. Tobe was sitting with his feet up on his desk—an act he could ill afford if the captain was present. He grinned when he saw it was Wes.

"It's about time—your supper's cold. Coffee's hot though. I built a little fire to take off the chill."

Wes helped himself to a cup and sat down to eat. When he had finished, he poured another cup and sipped it in quiet contentment. Tobe waited respectfully for him to speak.

"Aww—that was good. Thanks, Tobe. Did you get the note to my sister?"

"Sure did, Wes. She read it and cried. Then she kissed me on the cheek and ran to her room." Tobe's face shone as he related the details of how he had gotten her alone. Wes nodded his approval.

"Tobe, do you have someone we can trust to let you know when Cromwell breaks up his game and goes to his room? How about Abraham?"

"Good choice!" Tobe answered enthusiastically. "I'll look him up now. He may be over there. He sure likes that music. Look after things here. I'll be right back."

Waiting for Tobe to return, Wes occupied his mind by wondering what Lee was doing. His longing to talk to her revived, but he knew in his heart that he must first complete the task that lay ahead of him. The danger involved in helping Testa escape was very real, and he was aware that Cromwell would have no qualms about shooting either of them, then fleeing into the night.

The sound of rapid footsteps caught his attention. Wes jumped to his feet and waited, hands hanging free to his side. It was Tobe who entered, white faced, with eyes flashing in disbelief and anguish.

"Cromwell hasn't been seen all evening, neither has Testa! Abraham hadn't thought much about it until I asked him where they were."

Wes strode from the room and stalked across to the trading post. When he entered the smoke-filled room, no one paid much heed. Abraham was standing beside the piano listening intently to a young soldier who was playing. Over in the corner where Cromwell usually had his game going, some troopers were engaged in a friendly game of cards.

Pushing his way through the crowd, Wes went into the hall leading to the rooms in the back. The door to Cromwell's room was open and empty. The odor of stale cigar smoke was still in the room. He backed out and went to Testa's room. Feeling around he found a match and lit the candle he remembered being on the little table. The bed had not been used, and all her things were missing. That meant they had been gone for some time.

Wes took the candle and looked the room over closely, hoping that Testa might have left him some word of their whereabouts. He had about given up when he recalled that as a little girl Testa had always left notes under her pillow. Tossing the pillow aside, he found a small piece of paper and a stub of a pencil.

Wes. I have to hurry. We are . . .

The note was unfinished. She had probably been interrupted by Cromwell coming for her. Taking the candle, he let himself out the back door. Hoofprints in the dirt told the story. Then he saw something that caused him to catch his breath. There in the sand was a print that he had seen before. It was made by a hoof that bore a slightly crooked shoe on the right foreleg. The mare they had brought in with them had made that mark. His heart sank within him as he realized what that could mean. Questions crowded his mind. Had Webster gone with Cromwell? Would this explain his absence from their room? What about Lee? McDuggal would not have allowed her to leave the fort—if he had known.

The candle fell from nerveless fingers, leaving him in darkness as it hit the ground. A cold feeling of impending despair held him captive for a brief moment. Shaking it off with a deep, agonizing breath, Wes headed back to where Tobe was anxiously waiting.

"They've taken off, all right. From the hoofprints, there's six of them. Webster may have gone with them!" Wes related, as he strode through the hall with Tobe close on his heels.

It took Captain McDuggal a few minutes to answer the forceful knock on the door. His face showed his agitation at being disturbed in the middle of the night.

"What in—oh, it's you, Wes. What's going on?" he managed, agitation turning to surprise.

"Mac! Is Lee in her room?" Wes asked in alarm.

"She should be. Why?"

Wes filled him in on his findings and suspicions. Mary McDuggal appeared, wrapped in a robe.

"What's all the commotion about?" she asked.

"Wife, see if Angela is in her room while I get some clothes on."

Wes followed Mrs. McDuggal to the closed door of Lee's room. There was no response to their knock. Opening the door, they found the room empty. The neatly arranged bed had not been slept in.

"When did you see her last?" Wes asked, as Tobe joined them.

"It was at suppertime. She was cleaning up the rest of the dishes when her father came to take her for a walk. I didn't see them leave. I wasn't worried when it came bedtime, because I knew she was with her father."

"Oh dear, what do you think is wrong?" she asked, looking from Wes to Tobe.

"We think Mr. Webster has taken her and left the fort with some others."

Captain McDuggal returned dressed in his uniform, riding gloves in his hand.

"Mac, you'll have to do something—it's—"

"Now, Mary, don't you worry none. We'll do what we can. Corporal, get Lieutenant Berry here on the double, and see that my horse is ready. Hurry!"

When Tobe hesitated, the captain glared at him. "What is it, Corporal?"

"I'd like your permission to go, sir."

"All right, Corporal," Captain McDuggal granted with a wave of his hand. "Get a replacement to stay at your post."

Tobe scurried away, and Wes took his leave to get his rifle and saddlebags from his room. Soldiers were running to saddle up when he crossed to the stables for Rowdy. A light step fell in beside him.

"My brother is troubled," Red Hawk stated quietly.

"Yes, Red Hawk, my heart is heavy."

"It is the *pelo de oro?*"

"Yes," Wes answered, his voice breaking. "My sister is with them too."

"I go," Red Hawk declared, a glow in his somber eyes.

"But you are not well."

"I go," Red Hawk reiterated, stalking off in the dark.

14

*W*ES LED ROWDY FROM THE STABLE, stopping by the water trough to allow him to drink. "Better drink plenty, boy, it could be a long, dry ride."

When he got back to where Captain McDuggal was waiting, Red Hawk rode by on a spirited mustang. The dragoon of men fell into formation behind them.

"The way we figure it, Wes, they've got at least five or six hours on us. If they're ridin' slow because of the women, that'll help. I'll tell you right now, we've had a lot of Indian trouble out that way. We can only hope to overtake them before they are discovered and attacked. Let's go."

Once outside the gate, they started at a slow pace, waiting for Red Hawk to ride back with directions. They had gone about a mile when they came upon him.

"Stook zone," he said, using the Indian name for Tucson, which meant, water at foot of black mountain. "Ride fast!"

He whirled his horse and set off at a rapid gait, keeping it for hours. Wes rode alongside of Red Hawk, holding Rowdy to a matching stride. It would have been easy for the big chestnut to leave them all behind, but Wes knew the folly of that, for what could one man do against so many.

The clouds that had held on for most of the day were showing signs of breaking up. A few stars began to make their appearance in the predawn sky. The cool wind that had blown all day stung their cheeks.

Red Hawk put his hand up in a signal to halt, bringing his horse up short, causing everyone down the line to fight for control to keep from running into one another. Leaning forward in the saddle, a dark, intense figure, he listened to the sounds of the desert. He dismounted holding the reins of his fiery mount and placed his ear to the ground. With a grunt of satisfaction, he jumped astride the prancing horse.

"I ride—you stay! I be back!" Red Hawk commanded in gutteral tones, riding away to vanish in the night.

Wes stepped down from the saddle. Captain McDuggal gave the order to dismount and followed suit. The cavalrymen were more than glad for the opportunity to stretch their legs. However, there were no complaints, for most had volunteered to come. Conversation among them was subdued as each sensed the serious mission they were on.

Leading Rowdy a few steps ahead, Wes stood with his face turned toward the trail, eyes trying to penetrate the darkness for the returning scout. How far ahead were Lee and Testa, he wondered. Could they be camped near at hand? Was that the reason for Red Hawk's behavior? Could it be? He refused to allow himself to think about what may lie ahead. Surely, a merciful God would overshadow them with His protecting care.

"O God, please watch over them," he moaned. Anguish mounted in him as each precious moment passed. A great struggle raged in his mind. Through the years he had not been in the habit of praying as he ought. Even during the war years he had relegated the job to his mother, who had always assured him she was praying for his safety, as she would be at this moment. He had always been a believer, but unlike his mother, he had never been a devoted follower. So, why should God listen to him now?

Glad for the early morning darkness that surrounded him, hiding his face, Wes was as a twig bent in the wind, blown back and forth by the storm of doubt that assailed him. Fear for Lee and Testa filled him with a cold dread. He fought it off with all the inner strength afforded him. Lifting his eyes to the heavens, he prayed silently, first for Lee and Testa, then for himself. A calm assurance filled his heart, and he bowed his head in submission to God's will.

A warm hand grasped him on the shoulder. Captain McDuggal stood by his side for a moment in comforting silence before speaking with great feeling.

"I've seen some hard times on this western frontier, Wes, but none more difficult than this. Angela has become the daughter Mary and I never had. Life out here is especially hard on the womenfolk. We—we can only pray God will be merciful." His voice broke, and he turned away.

A staccato of hoofs announced Red Hawk's return. The men mounted, ready to move on. Rowdy held his head high, ears pointed in the incoming scout's direction, prancing in anticipation of action. The Indian pulled his horse up short.

"We must ride fast!" he cried, swinging his mustang in a wide circle and heading out at a full speed. The column of troops spurred their mounts into full gallop after him. There was no doubt in their minds of the urgency in the scout's demeanor. There were hostiles in the area.

Wes rode with the blood pounding in his temples and fear gripping his heart. "O God, please let us be in time," he gasped out loud.

When the first light of the morning came, Wes was surprised to find they had turned in a more southerly direction. Still, his trust in Red Hawk did not waver as they raced ahead. Though the ground beneath Rowdy's feet was a gray blur, the time drug slowly by. It was as if they were frozen in time on a treadmill of sand and cactus. The distant mountains wrapped in a somber gloom remained aloof.

Wes glanced over his shoulder at the men behind him. They rode as one, leaning low in their saddles, hats pulled down over their faces. His heart thrilled at the sight of them. Captain McDuggal rode on his right flank, his big horse trying to keep up with Rowdy's long stride. Their mounts were already showing signs of real fatigue. Wes realized they would not be able to keep up this pace long.

A break in Rowdy's gait drew his attention forward. Red Hawk had slowed to a walk, bringing his mustang to a halt. Wes pulled the big chestnut to a stop, sending a shower of dust on the guide who waited until all had stopped before speaking.

"We rest," he said, striding off to a high, boulder-strewn mound, leading his pony.

The men used the time to see to the care of their mounts. Wes fed Rowdy a few handfuls of oats and poured water into his hat for him to drink. The big horse drank gratefully. This done, he checked the cinches and stood waiting. He could see the Indian scout standing motionless, head bent slightly forward in a listening position. What a wild, magnificent figure he made with the red glow of the rising sun lighting up his dark, tawny skin.

As he watched, Wes saw him whirl and jump from rock to rock, surefooted as a mountain lion. He leaped into the saddle and came swiftly toward them, turning into the trail. Those waiting mounted up almost as one and quickly fell in behind him. Wes caught up with Red Hawk, who gave no notice of his presence, as once again they sped on toward the distant mountains.

The trail was more pronounced in the sandy soil now, and easy to follow. The miles passed slowly behind them as the gait of the horses lessened. When they came over a rise in the ground, Wes was surprised to find they had drawn closer to the mountain than he had realized. In the distance he could see a green patch of trees shining in the midday sun. The cool wind that had blown steady in the early morning had stopped, and it had grown still and hot.

Red Hawk slowed his tired horse to a walk, leading them into the shade of some mesquite trees lined along a dry stream bank. Tying his mustang to a tree limb, he shifted his rifle before speaking.

"I look. You wait."

"Red Hawk . . . wait!" Wes called after the scout who was taking off at a run. "Take Rowdy, he's still strong. You'll get there quicker."

The Indian stopped abruptly, turning a dark face to Wes. A soft gleam came into his eyes as he looked at the big chestnut.

"You trust me with most prized possession?"

"My most prized possessions are there in the desert, my brother," Wes answered in a strangled voice, dropping his head.

A strange, fierce shadow came over Red Hawk's countenance as he strode in a singular action to where Wes stood. Taking the reins from Wes, he laid a dark hand on his shoulder.

"See *pelo de oro,* soon," he said softly, and he jumped into the saddle and was gone, leaving a trail of dust rising into the air.

The men settled into the shade to rest, each with his rifle ready. Some stretched out on the sand, others leaned against the trees. Corporal Johnston sat off to one side with his face in his hands, a tense, distraught figure in a dust-ladened uniform. His hat lay on the ground beside him.

Wes felt his heart go out to this game young man. He had been so wrapped up in his own feelings, he had not thought about the anguish Tobe must be going through. He walked over to where he sat and hunkered down beside him, laying a hand on Tobe's arm.

"Are you all right, Tobe?"

Tobe lifted an ashen face to Wes. Red-rimmed eyes, glassy from lack of sleep, came into focus. In a futile effort he pushed the damp hair back from his forehead.

Wes repeated his question.

"It sure hurts—knowin' they're out there facing only God knows what, Wes," Tobe managed finally.

"I know, Tobe."

"How can you be so calm, Wes? Knowing what they may be going through this very minute."

"I've had my moments, too, Tobe. It helps to pray—although I have to admit, I've never done much of it. Mostly left it to the womenfolk. But this is different. Those girls need help, and God is the only one who can watch out for them until we get there. You will have to trust Him to overshadow them."

"That's the way it is, Mr. Tobe," Abraham chimed in encouragingly. "I've done a lotta praying since I left my mama's knee. That's what'll bring you through."

Tobe turned his head to find the black man speaking from under his hat, which he had pulled low to shade his face. Wes squeezed his arm and moved away to where Captain McDuggal lay dosing beneath a tree. Not wanting to awaken him, he stood watching the fading trail of dust. Wearily he sat down to wait among the snoring men who could no longer fight off the inevitability of sleep. Only Tobe and Abraham remained awake, each caught in his own thoughts.

The staccato sound of a running horse brought him to his senses. How long he had been asleep, Wes could only guess. He jumped to his feet to find that several of the troop had wakened to stand guard.

"Incoming rider!" someone called.

The whole camp became alert in an instant, gathering around their mounts in readiness. Tobe came to stand next to Wes and Captain McDuggal, holding the reins of his horse. All eyes were on the approaching horseman. Rowdy came on at a steady gait, then slowed to a walk as he came near.

Wes stepped out to meet him. "Come on, boy," he called, but his eyes were on the stoic countenance of Red Hawk who swayed in the saddle. His heart sank as the Indian slipped to the ground avoiding his unspoken question. Red Hawk turned to face the mountain. He ignored the order to report, given by Captain McDuggal.

"We will go—now!" he said, without turning.

15

WES BATTLED THE DREAD that tried to fill his heart as he rode the short distance to the mountain. Red Hawk's manner had led them all to believe there was little hope they would find the girls. Riding beside him now, Wes wondered what lay in store for them as they neared the inviting, shady coolness of the big cottonwood trees. The tracks they had been following were suddenly obliterated by the unshod hoofprints of Indian ponies.

He felt his blood run cold as he saw that they turned in the same direction as Cromwell's party. Judging by the sign, they were all traveling at a fast gait. The scout led them on until they reached the edge of the trees where he slid from his horse, waiting for all to dismount and secure their animals before leading them on.

"Apaches! Big fight!" he began, pointing to the arrows lodged in the trees. "All killed. Come."

In horror, they followed him into the bloody glade where they found the mutilated bodies of the men who remained where they had fallen. It was a sickening sight. Captain McDuggal quickly ordered guards posted and a burial detail to begin at once. The women were probably taken to face a worse fate.

Wes sank down on a log in despair. Wicked and murderous as he was, Cromwell had met a cruel and inhuman fate. Wes had seen men die in the war, but never anything like this. Suddenly, it dawned on him that he had not seen Webster's body among the dead in this area. Could it be, he was alive and the girls were with him?

Wes got to his feet, frantically looking around. Running here and there, he would fall on his hands and knees, crawling here and there. As Red Hawk and the Captain watched in sympathy, he gave a wild cry. There among the many tracks, he found a familiar hoofprint. He examined it carefully. The track led off to the right to vanish in a grassy area. He followed it to find it reappeared again on the other side. Red Hawk joined him and ran ahead, crouching low as he went.

"Come!" he gestured to Wes, then ran forward to a crevice in the rocks.

Wes hurried forward to find Webster lying on his back, an arrow protruding from his chest. But, his body bore none of the marks of brutality afforded the others. With hope crushed, Wes sat wondering about this. Red Hawk continued to study the ground.

"Look," Red Hawk grunted excitedly.

He straightened, looking around him. Then he walked in a circle looking closely at the soil and checking for broken twigs. He came again to where Wes waited. Curiously, he paused at a small, round dent in the sand at the end of Webster's outflung arm. His dark eyes were lit with a strange fire. Uttering a strange cry, he almost upset Wes as he brushed him aside. Falling on one knee, the faithful scout pointed at a small footprint.

"Pelo de oro!"

Wes felt the ground sway beneath him as his blurred eyes tried to focus on the small imprint in the ground. He groped as a man gone blind. When his vision cleared, he saw the clear outline of a woman's foot. When had it been made? By some miracle, would they still be here?

Red Hawk helped him to his feet, where he staggered like a drunken man. Hope sprung alive in him once more. Still unsteady on his feet, he somehow stayed beside the scout whose hawklike gaze scoured the ground. The prints led past where Cromwell had been slain and on to the spring on the other side. They were clearly defined in the mud by the water hole.

"*Pelo de oro* took canteen—came here for water."

Red Hawk got to his feet and looked up into the rocks but saw nothing. With Wes at his side, he turned back in the direction they had come, pausing every little bit to stare up the mountain. The tracks had disappeared in the rocky litter.

"We search—you go—I go—we meet," Red Hawk said, sweeping his arms in a wide circle.

Wes worked his way back to where they had found Cromwell. A narrow passage went up into the rocks above. Working his way up he spotted something white fluttering in the sun. His pulse quickened and his breath came in short gasps as he ran up the path.

He rounded the rock to find Lee and Testa lying side by side. A canteen lay between them. In one hand Lee clutched the cross that had been her father's. There was dried blood on her fair face. Testa was on her back, a blood-soaked bandage on her breast. Wes hesitated, fearing they might be dead. As he stepped forward, he dislodged a rock that rattled loudly down the path.

Lee jumped to her feet swiftly as a cat, aiming the concealed gun at Wes. Her eyes were wild with fear.

"Don't you come any closer!" she cried shrilly, the heavy weapon weaving back and forth in her hand as she pulled the hammer back.

"Lee, it's Wes—I've—I've come to help you," he said, reaching out to her as he stepped forward.

"Stop! Don't take another step. I saw you kill those men! You will not get me! I'll shoot myself."

Wes stood rooted to the spot. Lee was in shock and did not recognize him. Judging the distance between them, he realized it would be foolhardy to go any closer. He would not be able to reach her before she fired the revolver, ending her life. She remained motionless and resolute, her golden hair falling over her white face. From the corner of his eye, he saw Red Hawk coming up the hill behind her. He would have to stall for time.

"How long have you been here?" he asked calmly.

She did not answer but continued to watch him warily, a tense, poised figure, ready to react.

"Is the other girl dead?" he started again.

"I think so. I tried to save her. He loves her. If he would have been here, he would have known what to do. I couldn't stop the bleeding." She began to cry, swaying back and forth.

Red Hawk was just a few steps from her now. If only he would hurry. As he edged ever nearer a twig snapped under his foot.

Lee whirled like a tigress, pulling the trigger, but the hammer fell on an empty chamber. She struggled to cock the gun again, but Red Hawk caught her and held her tight. With a despairing sob, she fell limp in his arms. Carefully he lowered her to the ground, taking the weapon away. Wes expelled a deep breath and bounded to her side. Tenderly, he gathered her in his arms and held her to his chest, burying his face in her hair, unashamed of the tears that ran down his face.

"*Pelo de oro* safe now, my brother," Red Hawk murmured.

A low moan startled them both. It had come from Testa. She was still alive!

"Red Hawk, get some help up here. Tell Tobe. Hurry!"

It was needless to urge the Indian to be quick, for he was already leaping down through the rocks.

When he returned, he was accompanied by Captain McDuggal, Tobe, and another trooper who had a small black bag in his hand. Wes turned Lee over to the captain who held her in his arms, soothing her as he would a baby, eyes wet with tears.

Tobe had fallen to his knees and was calling to Testa, confessing his love for her.

"Step aside, son, I need to take care of that wound," said the soldier whom Wes had not met before.

Wes took Tobe and led him away. "Sit here. I'll call you when we're through," he said gently and turned away to help.

"Wes," Tobe importuned, grabbing his arm, "how do we pray?"

"It's easy, Tobe, just bow your head and talk to God about what's troubling you," Wes answered, leaving him there.

It didn't take long to tend to Testa's needs. Now it was in God's hands. She had lost a lot of blood. They would have to remain where they were until she was well enough to make the long trip back.

* * *

The day had been unusually warm in the desert for November. To escape the oppressive heat in his small quarters, Wes sat in the open door. It had been a week since they had returned from their rescue mission. Every day he had gone to see how Testa was progressing, always with the hope that he would be able to see Lee and talk with her. Whether by chance or by choice, she seemed to be busy elsewhere.

Mary McDuggal was very gracious to him, letting him stay with his sister as long as he wished. The long trip back had been hard on her. Though she was conscious, she was still too weak to talk. The few times he had found Testa awake, her dark eyes, which had been so full of life, were dull and listless. She would fix them on his face in an uncomprehending stare until she fell asleep again.

Wes was much relieved when the physician at the post had assured him Testa was out of danger. She had been so frail and spent that the loss of blood had taken its toll. It would take time, but she would be all right.

He had sought out Tobe earlier in the day to tell him the good news. The young man had returned to his duties but remained somber and quiet. It was good to see the joy and hope come alive in him again.

As the sun sank lower in the west, the plaintive note of the bugler sounded taps, announcing the end of another day in the life of the fort. A light step preceded Red Hawk's appearance around the corner. He had come every evening, sitting quietly, listening to conversations if someone happened by to see Wes. Wes was glad to have the company. But tonight it was hard to shake the dejection that had settled over him. There was a long silence between them, broken finally by the scout.

"You troubled, my brother?"

Wes dropped his head, staring long at his worn boot rather than face Red Hawk's piercing gaze. How could he tell this friend of a futile love, discovered too late.

"The Raven Hair—*pelo de oro*, all right?"

"Yes, Red Hawk, Testa is getting better. I haven't seen Lee since we got back."

Red Hawk studied his friend's face, then turned his gaze to the brilliant horizon before speaking again.

"You trouble here," he indicated, pointing to his heart. "It is the *pelo de oro* you long for." He stood to his feet in one agile movement. "She will come," he prophesied, stalking away in the dark, leaving Wes to ponder his last remark.

It was late when he sought his bed. Satisfied that he had thought things through, he decided that there was no reason for him to remain here at the fort any longer than necessary. As soon as Testa was strong enough to travel, he would take her home. The McDuggals would see that Lee was cared for.

The thought of going home did not bring the anticipation it once did. Even as he tried to recall the pleasant times with Colonel Stothard and the men he rode with, a face framed with golden hair prevented him. Turning and tossing in his bed, he was confronted with the fact that he could not leave Lee. Going back would be to face a life of emptiness without her. Hours passed before he fell into a troubled sleep.

16

*W*EARY IN BODY, Angela Lee sought her bed early. She had helped Mrs. McDuggal wash and replace the curtains, along with the constant care of Testa, who shared the room with her. The small lamp on the table cast a dim light against the opposite wall.

Testa moved restlessly, her arms flailing the air. "Noooo!" she moaned. "No, don't hit me any more, please," she whispered.

Angela went to her side. Speaking in soothing tones she tried to quiet the tormented girl as she bathed her face with water and gave her a drink.

"Wes. Where are you Wes? Please—come for me, Wes, before it's too late!" Testa pleaded.

"Shhh! Wes is here. He loves you and will take care of you," Angela crooned, stroking the hair from Testa's forehead.

"Will mother forgive me, Wes? Will she? When we were kids, you were always—the good one. I always thought she loved—you best."

Angela sat in stunned silence as Testa babbled on. Was this girl whose picture Wes carried in a locket his sister? Dare she ask?

"Testa, who is Wes?" Angela asked, her voice sounding faint as the blood pounded in her temples.

"Wes—my brother. Is he here? Did he come—after all?"

"Yes, he is here. He has come to take you home. Now rest so you will get strong," Angela Lee said softly, her heart pounding with joy.

Long after Testa had fallen asleep, Angela Lee lay awake staring at the ceiling of her tiny room. When she had regained consciousness there on the mountain, she was cradled in Captain McDuggal's arms. Wes was leaning over Testa helping the doctor with the wound. From that point on he had paid little attention to her except to inquire about her welfare. He and Tobe had taken turns carrying Testa home in their arms.

She had avoided any personal contact with Wes, hoping it would make it easier to still the tumult in her heart at the very sight of him. She had lost weight, and dark circles under her eyes made her look pale and wan. The McDuggals allowed it was due to the terrible experience she had gone through.

Recalling the night that seemed so long ago, she remembered what Wes must have been trying to say when she fled from the room. When she had accused him of loving the girl in the locket, he could not deny it because he did love his sister. What a terrible, selfish mistake she had made. No wonder he stayed his distance from her. What tangled webs human beings spin, ensnaring themselves in the errors of their own ways.

Tears bathed her eyes as she faced the fact there was little reason to hope that Wes loved her. Yet, when she remembered his words to her in the wagon that night, it caused her heart to swell.

Sleep refused to come as she lay torn between hope and despair. Out on the prairie, she heard the mournful sound of a coyote, calling to its mate. If only it would be that easy! Tomorrow, she vowed, when Wes came to see Testa, she would be there. Perhaps—oh, what should she say. Ohh! Tormented by her own self doubt, she buried her face in the pillow.

It was Mary McDuggal's knock at her door the next morning that awakened her. Surprised she had fallen asleep, Angela Lee quickly responded to the call for breakfast. Dipping water from a bucket into a small bowl, she washed her face. The water cooled her burning eyes. Hurriedly she dressed with trembling fingers. An unsmiling image in the small mirror mocked her as she brushed the tangles from her hair. Dropping her arms to her side, she stared at the reflection in the glass. The restless night had wreaked havoc in her face, deepening the shadows in her eyes, making them appear even more luminous. She turned away with a sigh to straighten her small bed. When she fluffed her pillow her hand came in contact with the gold cross she had taken from her father's hand. Picking it up, she recalled the first time she had seen it. Her mother had given it to her pastor-husband when Angela Lee was five years of age. Now, holding it in her hand, she felt comforted. She looked up to find Testa curiously watching her.

"Who—are you?" she asked wearily.

"I am the one who was on the mountain with you. My father and I were in your party when we were attacked. I took care of you as best I could. My name is Angela Lee. Do you need something?"

"A drink of water."

Angela Lee held the glass to Testa's lips, waiting until she had taken several sips before speaking again.

"You are better. Perhaps the doctor will let you sit up a little today. Are you hungry?" When Testa nodded, Angela Lee expressed her approval.

"Good! I will bring you some breakfast soon."

"Well, here's our sleepyhead, Mary," Captain McDuggal exclaimed by way of greeting to Angela Lee as she entered the small kitchen.

"Lands sake, child! It was like raisin' the dead this morning," Mary McDuggal chimed in cheerfully. She rose to get the plate of food she had in the warmer. Setting it before her young guest, she noted the deepened shadows of weariness in the youthful face.

"Eat hearty now, you haven't been eating enough to keep a bird alive."

"Thank you. I—I'll try. It smells good," Angela replied, surveying the plate of food before her. "Our patient is much better this morning. The fever is gone, and she seems more herself. Said she was hungry. That's a good sign. I told her I would bring her something."

"You just sit there and eat, Angela. I'll go see to her," Mrs. McDuggal reiterated, leaving the room.

Captain McDuggal pushed his plate aside and sat watching Angela as she picked at her food.

"Red Hawk says Wes isn't doing so well," he ventured after a period of silence.

"Oh, is he sick?" Angela asked, alarm in her voice.

"Says he stays to himself except to go see his horse. Evenings he just sits there at his quarters mooning away. Won't hardly talk. The scout says his problem is in here," the captain continued, pointing to his chest.

"His heart?"

"It seems a certain young lady is ignoring him and it's breaking his heart. Poor man. That's too bad."

He got up from the table and reached for his hat, noting the blaze of color that had invaded her face. He took his leave, feeling satisfied he had said enough.

No longer hungry, Angela picked up the plates, scraped and washed them. All the while her mind was in a whirl. When the last dish was dried and stacked in the crude cupboard, she stood staring out the window at the distant mountains. Hope that had been repressed by doubt and fear burst forth again, filling her with wild abandonment.

Unsteadily she walked to the little sitting room where she sank into a chair. Laying her head back she succumbed to the joy and rapture of a woman in love. Her heart felt as if it would burst!

"If you think you have heart troubles now, Mr. Scott, you just wait until this evening," she vowed out loud with a blushing face.

Hearing Mrs. McDuggal return to the kitchen, Angela Lee went out to see if she could be of help. She was informed Testa had eaten a fair breakfast and was now asleep. Her heart was singing as she assisted with the laundry. Mary McDuggal saw the change in Angela Lee's demeanor but wisely kept her silence, sure that her husband had been up to his matchmaking again. Whatever had wrought the change, she was glad to see it.

Angela Lee offered to hang the clothes on the line, mainly to get some fresh air and to have time to herself to think. She was so engrossed in her thoughts she had not noticed Red Hawk's approach. It startled her when he spoke so closely behind her.

"*Pelo de oro* looks pale. You well?"

She turned quickly to find him standing there, head erect, dark, somber gaze alight with a warm glow. He was dressed in buckskin, and beaded moccasins encased his feet.

"Yes, I am well, Red Hawk."

"How is other girl?"

"She is much better today."

When he did not speak again, but stood there watching her, she grew uncomfortable. She finished hanging the last pieces of clothing and picked up the basket to go in. He held up his hand to stop her.

"My brother is no good. Hurt here," he said stoically, gesturing toward his heart. "You come now?"

"No, Red Hawk, I will come at evening. Please do not tell him I am coming."

He nodded. "You come."

He turned and strode swiftly away, leaving her to stand there wondering.

"Dear me, how many more are going to tell me how miserable Wes is? He hasn't been the only one! Well, it appears I am the only heart doctor in the fort," she sighed, flipping her golden hair back over her shoulders.

Testa was sitting up in a chair when she returned. Her hair, which had been washed and brushed, shone like a raven's wing. Though she looked very thin, there was more color in her face. Her black eyes expressed her pleasure to have company for a while.

"Would you like me to read to you?"

"Y-yes."

"There are some books in the sitting room. I'll get one."

Angela Lee chose a book of poetry and went back to where Testa sat waiting. They were interrupted a short time later by Mrs. McDuggal, who had a merry twinkle in her eye.

"There's a young man out here who has been asking about you every day, Testa. I told him he could visit you for a few minutes, if you feel up to it. Do you?" she asked cheerfully.

Testa nodded her head, eyes lighting up. Angela Lee closed her book and laid it aside. Slipping from the room, she gave an encouraging smile to Tobe, whose presence seemed to fill the tiny room. She settled into a chair in the quiet of the parlor, listening to the murmur of their voices, followed by periods of silence. She had known that Corporal Johnston was very much in love with Testa. She had seen evidence of his devotion out on the mountain. But she was not sure of Testa's interest in Tobe until she saw her face when he entered the room.

Her pulse stirred as her mind went to her own promised encounter with Wes. This was the second day he had not come to see Testa. Somehow she knew he would not come. Her coolness and total disregard of his presence had hurt and confused him. But what about her? No one had bothered to tell her that Testa was his sister, not even Wes. Perhaps they assumed that she knew since she had spent time with her on that fateful trip. She had suppressed her love and kept her distance out of respect for Wes's feelings. After all, she reasoned in defense of herself, wasn't that another proof of her devotion? So deeply was she engrossed in her thoughts she did not hear Mrs. McDuggal call her name.

"Angela, are you all right, dear?"

The concern in this kind woman's face touched her heart, bringing the tears so close to the surface. All the pent-up emotion and stress that had lay hidden for so long was released.

"There, there—you just go ahead and have a good cry," Mary McDuggal comforted in a soothing voice, putting her arms around the distraught girl. "You've got an awful lot bottled up in you that needs to come out. When you're empty, God will come in and fill that void with peace."

When at last her sobs subsided, Angela Lee felt a calm assurance replace the turmoil that had been in her heart for so long. Gone was all the bitterness she had harbored against the people of the church who had asked them to leave. Gone was the disillusionment she had felt toward her father. She remembered the words he had spoken that last morning here, "God will be our 'shadow from the heat.'"

"Thank you, Mother McDuggal, for your kindness and understanding," she said with feeling, bringing joy to the childless woman's heart. "I'll be fine now."

"There's Testa calling. You see what she needs, and I'll start supper," suggested the older woman, releasing her with a pat on the shoulder.

Drying her tears, Angela Lee went to find that Tobe had left and a weary Testa was wanting to lie down again. She assisted the emotionally spent girl back to her cot and straightened the covers around her. All the while Testa's questioning eyes did not leave her tear-stained face.

"Why hasn't Wes come to see me?"

"I don't know, Testa, perhaps you ought to ask Captain McDuggal," Angela Lee answered, avoiding her solemn gaze.

"Tobe said he's sick." When no reply was forthcoming, Testa went on. "He said Wes has been staying at his quarters, moping around and staring off toward the mountains. That he just hasn't been himself since we returned to the fort. Tobe says Wes is terribly in love with you. Do you love my brother?"

Angela sank trembling to the side of the bed and took Testa's thin white hand in hers. With words tumbling over one another, she told her all that had happened up to her promised visit tonight.

Testa listened with rapt expression. "Oh, how I would like to be a little mouse and be there to see Wes's face!" she exclaimed, giving Angela's hand a squeeze.

"Angela, can you keep a secret?" Testa asked, after a moment's silence, her black eyes shining like stars.

"Yes, Testa, what is it?"

"Tobe has asked me to marry him . . . and I said yes!"

"Oh, Testa, I'm so happy for you!" Angela Lee responded, hugging her. "Tobe is such a fine young man, and you will make him a good wife. That's wonderful."

Captain McDuggal came in early and stopped by the door where the girls were. Taking in the happy scene, his gray eyes twinkled and a broad smile swept across his countenance, replacing the sternness usually reserved for the troops.

"Well, well, now that's better. I'm sure glad to see the landscape changing around here. I was kinda gettin' worried about all the doom and gloom. Corporal Johnston passed me in the hall awhile ago and didn't even see me. He looked like he was walkin' on air. I don't guess you would know anything about that would you, Testa?" he teased.

Testa hid her blushing face in the pillow.

"Haw! Haw! It's good to see a little happiness taking place in this drab old fort. Now, if we can just figure out what to do about a certain young man that's got heart trouble, things might go smooth around here for a while." His amused gaze rested on Angela Lee, bringing a rosy hue to her cheeks.

She was relieved when he wandered off to hunt his wife, leaving them alone. Testa fell asleep, leaving her to her own resources. Time passed slowly as excitement built up inside her. She tried to read but couldn't concentrate. Glad when the call to supper came, she found that she could scarcely swallow her food.

"You're awfully quiet tonight, Angela," the Captain observed.

Angela Lee faced him with a grave face. She laid her fork down so that he would not notice her trembling hands.

"I'm going to see Wes this evening. Could you tell me where he is staying?"

"Better yet, to keep you from being mobbed by those woman-hungry troops out there, I'll escort you. Since you girls have been here I think every trooper in my command has been in my office for some vague reason or another. It's been hard to run the business of the fort."

"Let me know when you're ready," he concluded, pushing his plate back.

"It's growing dark; could we leave right away?"

"It will be cool. I'll get you a shawl," Mary McDuggal offered, leaving to get it.

When Angela came from her room the captain had donned his jacket and stood waiting. Accepting the shawl Mrs. McDuggal held out to her, she followed him out. He paused on the front step for her to take his arm, and together they walked across the parade ground. Many envious eyes followed them. From the porch of the trading post, two scouts watched with interest. One sat on a wooden bench, his white head nodding in consent, the other stood aside, arms crossed, dark eyes glowing.

Captain McDuggal stopped at the door of a darkened room. "Wes, are you in there?"

"Yes, Mac, come on in," came the somber reply.

"I'll go in first," the captain whispered in her ear, "better make sure he's dressed decent enough. Wait here."

Angela Lee backed into the shadows, her legs suddenly becoming so weak she found it necessary to lean against the building to support herself.

"Heard you've been sick. What's the matter with you?"

"Nothing!" Wes exploded. "Good heavens, Mac! Can't a fella work on his own problems without everyone interfering!" His feet hit the floor with a loud thump as he sat up. He lit the candle on the table with a trembling hand, then turned to glare at his friend.

"You look terrible, Wes!"

"I'm sorry, Mac. I—I'll be all right. Can't you see I just want to be left alone?" Wes muttered, dropping his head in his hands.

"All right, Wes, let me know if you need anything."

No answer came as Captain McDuggal turned and walked out the door.

"He's all yours," he said softly, walking away.

Angela Lee peeped in the door. Wes was still sitting with his hands over his face. Summoning all the courage she could muster, she stepped into the room and moved hesitantly to stand before him.

"Mac, I told you to leave me alone—I—," Wes muttered despondently.

"Wes, it's Lee," she said tremulously, touching his hair.

She heard his breath catch in his throat, and his head jerked up in disbelief and wonder. She was shocked to see how haggard and hollow-cheeked his face appeared. Bravely she went on.

"I came to tell you that I love you and I don't ever want to be apart from you again."

"Lee! My dearest Lee!" he cried, jumping to his feet to gather her in his arms, burying his face in her fragrant hair. "Lee, I thought I had lost you—out on the mountain—I couldn't bear it! Red Hawk helped me—he saw your track— I didn't want to live without you. Oh, Lee, God spared you—I believe it—I asked Him—and He did it! You dear, brave girl. My darling Angel."

He held her at arm's length where he could look into her face. There he saw all the glory of a woman's love. Taking her by the hand, he led her to the door.

"Come—for your sake—we will not remain here. What will those who saw you come think? We'll walk and talk."

"Wait!" Angela Lee laid a hand on his arm, detaining him. "Why did you stay away from me there on the mountain? I needed you so. I didn't know Testa was your sister. She kept calling your name. When you carried her back on your horse, I thought she was the one you loved. No one told me."

He drew her into his arms again. "You've been the only one I have loved. I was afraid I would be killed when I faced Cromwell to rescue Testa, so I couldn't tell you that night when you came to me. I didn't think it was fair to you. After you reacted the way you did, I wasn't sure. In my own blind way, I didn't realize I had hurt you so. When I finally figured it out, you were gone.

"You were unconscious when I held you in my arms after finding you on the mountain. When Testa moaned, letting us know she was alive, I turned you over to Mac while I helped the doctor. After that I didn't trust myself. I didn't want to take advantage of you after what you had been through."

"My darling Wes," Angela Lee murmured as she held her lips to his.

Releasing her, he led her out into the starlit night where they walked, arms entwined.

From the shadows behind them, Red Hawk watched and thought of the dusky-eyed Indian maiden that lay beneath the sod of a windswept prairie far away.